MW01181925

Amanda

A HEART COMES HOME

BETTY LOWREY

Copyright © 2022 by Betty Lowrey.

ISBN: 978-1-0880-5792-6

All rights reserved. No part of this book may be reproduced or transmitted in any form or by any means, electronic or mechanical, including photocopying, recording, or by any information storage and retrieval system without express written permission from the author, except in the case of brief quotations embodied in critical reviews and certain other non-commercial uses permitted by copyright law.

PROLOGUE

I t was going to be a wonderful Christmas. She had prayed this one would be better. The stigma of her parent's divorce had lived in her heart all these years but now, building a home would fill the void. She was the happiest girl in the world! Clark had popped the question in a most endearing way and tonight they were celebrating their engagement. "I'll bring your ring," he said and she found the promise carried her through the day. She was to meet him, and she arrived first. The musicians came to the table, three men and a woman, but it was the woman that made her uneasy. Clark was also a musician, on the side, perhaps that was a conflict. The woman leaned in to say, "Do not marry him. He is dangerous. Take my word, I know. If you have any doubts, look in the next room, there is his son." Seeing the child, broke her heart. Clark could not deny the boy. He was the image of his father, a handsome lad, but sad. She waited, hoping some sense would come. But the woman's last words could not be forgotten, "Get out, he is dangerous." It was the following week, he appeared for work, drunk beyond sensibility, ridiculing and shaming her before the crew. "You aren't good enough for me," he said. "Did you really think I'd buy you a ring? You have to prove yourself." She left before dawn, the next day. The music on the radio made her sad. She turned to talk radio to find a doctor speaking on Stalking. She listened to keep her mind off her own problems.

Hello: I'm Dr. Mabry Lowenstein and tonight we are discussing by popular request, STALKING. That's right. Stalking. You have asked why people stalk others, are male or female more likely to stalk, and what can be done about it.

"Let's begin with why people stalk. Most who come to me for help are obsessed with the person they are stalking, whether infatuation, a lost love, or an ex-family member. Who stalks falls in society's different categories, as we mentioned the former partner, celebrity caliber, an acquaintance, such as a neighbor or a co-worker or maybe a television newscaster one sees every night or perhaps someone a person admires and lusts after. You say, well that's a lot of people. Yes, it is. But Stalking, is what it is; when the obsession to do so controls the person instead of the person controlling the obsession. Is Stalking dangerous? "Sometimes. If the Stalker wants harm to come to the object of the stalking, yes, it can be unto death. About one point three percent of all person's age sixteen or older were victims of stalking, last year," the doctor said. "And sometimes the stalker kills the victim he says he loves."

Stalking was the last thing in the world she needed to dwell on. She'd cried enough tears without the gory details of a crime about to happen. Thank God, she did not need to know that. Oh, she wished she hadn't turned the dial from music to talk shows. Now she tried to shut down her own mind.

Sometimes it starts with telling a person, no, you don't agree with them and they can't stand rejection," the woman said. Something made her feel uneasy about Clark.

Chapter

1

....

She drove all night, crying in sync with the rain falling on the windshield. She had left the state line in the early morning hours, as she had left the sleepy little town before it awakened. No one knew she was gone. Now, hours later and completely exhausted, coming into a new town she read the sign, population 1,163,000; a lot more people than where she lived the last three years. A flashing green arrow pointed to a motel. The lights were on inside, but she didn't see anyone at the desk. Snow flakes were falling but she hoped they quit; she had miles to go.

There was no way she could miss the dangling bulbs of tree lights, a reminder that Christmas had passed and a new year was dawning. Stratigically placed around the door, a symbol of Christmas past, they had fallen and some of the bulbs were missing. A messy invite to business she was thinking. Pulling her purse from the stack of papers thrown into the front seat she eased out of the car, walked the distance and went in. The door had a creepy bell like sound she supposed meant to alert whoever was supposed to be taking reservations... No one appeared. She tapped the bell on the riser in front of the desk but still no one appeared. Finally, she stepped to the door and called toward the back of the building.

"Is anyone here?" There was no reply. "Well, the door was open," she said to herself. She banged on the door that led to the back. "I need a room. Do you hear?" There was sound of a piece of furniture scraping on the floor, then quiet. "Do you have a room? Your arrow is flashing."

"Coming," a burly voice called back. "Don't wake the others."

She wondered what that meant but she didn't ask. A heavy-set man came down the hall, zipping his trousers and by the time he stood behind the desk had his shirt buttoned.

"What kind of room do you need? King or Queen? Inside the hall or with an outside entrance? Sixty dollars inside the hall, eighty with an outside door." He leaned on the riser studying her, no doubt wondering if she had the money. "Pay now."

While he wondered about her, she took in the Christmas tree, still standing, and wondered if they had the same kind of Christmas. Maybe we have more in common than he will ever know, but then his life might be good while all the effort I've put into mine has gone down the drain.

He was waiting. She gave him her card and he did the usual scan. He started to stick the card in the drawer of the old cash register. "Huh, uh, I can't leave my card with you."

"Then there's no room," he said and hand her the card.

"Fine with me," she replied and turned toward the door.

"Hey, wait up, I was just kidding."

She turned and gave him a dirty look. "It's late to be kidding about something like this and I'd think if you're going to sleep on the job, just maybe you should lock the front door. Do I have a room or not?"

"You have a room." He sounded resigned to the fact. "Where you from?"

"Out of town."

"Uh, huh. Where you headed?"

"Across the bridge."

"Uh, huh. Follow me."

"Where?"

"Down the hall." He handed her a sheet of paper. "That's your receipt. I put you inside, seems you are traveling alone and this ain't the best area to stay in."

At least they agreed on one thing. "So, you leave the door unlocked every night?"

He started a shuffle down the hall. "Not usually, got a sick wife, got side tracked and forgot."

A bit apprehensive, she followed wondering if he was lying when a woman's voice called out, "James, I need you. I can't do this by myself."

"You want to go on alone, or wait a minute for me?"

"I'll wait. You won't be long, will you?"

"Shouldn't. Gotta put her back on the bed, she's too weak to get there herself." He felt her question. "She has to sit up ever so often, even on oxygen she can't breathe. She thinks it helps." Amanda knew she cared but she was so tired she had nothing to say. She heard him grunt, a woman's low cry and a soft thud, no doubt as she landed on a soft mattress and then he was back breathing hard but ready to escort her down the hall. "She ain't well," he said. "She's gonna die. Breakfast across the street in the morning, just give them your tab, we'll pay. It's good food."

He opened a door to room 1-10. She stood on the outside, looking in. It wasn't bad. The tile was clean enough, where she'd expected a dirty rug, maybe green shag and was dreading that. With him still there she approached the bed, moved one of the pillows and turned back the coverlet to inspect the sheets. They were clean, but not ironed. She stooped to smell the pillow. A mistake. Anyway, she thought, the sheets are clean, no bedbugs detected.

Turning to face him, she said, "I'm okay. I'll probably check out in the morning. It's according to how I feel. I've just driven ten hours today."

"Georgia," he guessed.

"North Carolina."

He was padding back down the hall.

In the bathroom she found the towels, select the right size and went back to drape it over the pillow that had an oily smell from too much use or one greasy overnight guest. Kicking off her shoes she lay back wondering if anyone realized she was gone and especially would he know?

Clark Benson, tall, handsome and mean hearted, the pipe dreams every woman has and she had fallen for him. He could lie better than any man she'd ever listened to, and there were many in that category. Clark was the answer to any woman's dream, to walk down the street on his arm was heaven, with all the girl's gawking and women changing the path they meant to travel to pass by Clark. If I'm lyin,' I'm dyin. Almost, she sit up, but tiredness pinned her to the bed. She was hallucinating, saying those stupid silly words the young girls used when they saw Clark. It was the hours. She must get her suitcase…but to lay here just five minutes would help.

She awoke the next morning to the sound of doors opening and shutting with a bang as suitcases hit the wall and then wheeled on down the hall. Voices rose and swelled as people greet each other and she, with a horrible taste in her mouth realized she had wrapped her body in the dingy unwashed coverlet from the bed, her head on the towel draped pillow and she was fully dressed, something she never did was sleep in her clothes. Neither was she accustomed to driving ten hours in one day just to get away from people and the embarrassment Clark caused. Rising, she threw the comfort back in place and stalked out of the room angry with herself. Why couldn't she quit thinking of him? He was the biggest lie of her life and she thought her parents' divorce the worst even if her mother forgave her dad when it was really his fault. It was the months he let her think her mom was the one betrayed them all. Being the baby of the family wasn't easy. And then when he decided to marry Bertha, he had to come clean.

"It was my fault, Amanda," he yelled. "What do you want me to do?"

"Bring Mommie home and straighten up," she said through clenched teeth. She knew before she answered he wasn't going to do that. She was thirteen years old and had been going between the two for three years. She hated it. She was old enough to make a choice and she chose her old bedroom upstairs. Coming home, leaving the cramped one-bedroom flat in town she shared with her mother. "But I'll not abandon you," she promised her mother. "I can tell I get on your nerves, if I go there, you'll have room to breathe and I…well, it's home. It's not Dad, the reason I'm going…Mom, if Dad's got someone, maybe you'd like to find…it's hard to say, Mom, but I know you're lonely."

"For your dad, Amanda," her mother replied, softly.

There it was, the sadness she felt and the rebellion. She'd rebelled when Dad brought Bertha home. He had called to tell her, as though he were saying, "I'm bringing pizza, or apple pie." No, it was, "Hey, Mandy, I'm bringing Bertha home with me."

"No, Dad."

"What do you want me to do with her? Take her back? We're married." And she'd heard Bertha laugh, but she wasn't laughing when she came upstairs that night to see her new step daughter.

"I'm going to do my best to be friends with you, Amanda. I know you are hurting."

"You are the reason my father and Mother are divorced," Amanda spit out. "I don't like you."

"You don't know me, Honey, and I don't know you." Bertha turned to go down the stairs.

"Don't you ever call me honey. You don't have the right. You destroyed our home."

There was fire in her father's eye when he came up. "I think we've taught you better than to be disrespectful," he said through clenched teeth. "If you act that way again, you can pack your bags and go back to your mother."

"You don't have to worry about that, Dad. I'll go tonight."

"I'm not driving you," he'd said. "I'm truly disappointed in you."

"How do you think I feel. This is the home I grew up in. Because you couldn't control yourself and act like a husband and a father is supposed to, my mother...your real wife lives in a one room apartment with barely room to turn around and you bring your bar maid here to be the woman of the house."

That's when he slapped her; hard enough she fell back on the bed and whether from anger or remorse he turned and went down stairs. That was when she realized Bertha had stood at the foot of the stairs and heard the whole conversation. To this day, she decided he was still angry and remorse played no part in any of it. She packed her suitcase, grabbed her book bag and the most important essentials she thought she'd need and started walking the three miles in to town. It was the last half mile a farmer stopped to pick her up and delivered her to her mother's door.

"Aren't you Charles and Phyllis Lanis girl?" He had a boy she'd seen at school sitting in the passenger seat of the truck and the boy didn't say a word. She had nodded. He could see her in the visor mirror. "What's your name?" He'd ask and to her reply he'd said, "I'm glad to meet you, Amanda. I've known your parents all my life. They're fine people." On those words she'd just stared out the window. It had seemed he'd hated to leave her and had waited until her mother opened the door to let her in.

"Sweetie," Mom asked, "What are you doing here?"

"Dad kicked me out."

Phyllis appeared surprised. "Uhh…I can hardly imagine dad kicking you out. You and Dad?"

"I know," she'd said. She did know. She and Dad were close, as close as a girl is with her mother. But she hadn't gone back to live there, not when he ask her a hundred times. Dad and Bertha had the house to themselves. Holidays, birthdays, you name it, even at church she avoided them. She felt her family was the laughing stock of the community. Who goes to church with his new wife on his arm when the old wife, not even forty years old, is sitting at the piano?

But this was a new year and she was grown and mom was still trying to move on and doing a poor job of it because she still loved him. Phyllis words rang in her ears. "Baby, you have got to turn loose, if I can, you can." And why in the world am I thinking of all those past problem years when so much water has run under the bridge and I'm living my own night mare. Let's just review those little tidbits. She had held a bit of the resentment, enough to say, "you'll know when this heart comes home." Somehow, she had gotten through high school, two years of college on grants and after that couldn't find a job, other than helping out with Miss Jane, down at Husey's Accounting Service.

"Miss Amanda Lanis," Mr. Husey would say, "You just need to forget those lofty ideas for your future. Your future's right here in Jericho. Anyone as good as you with figures; your job is secure," She could still here his southern drawl. "Right Hea-uh." So, on the side she helped Miss Patty down at the flower shop and found her real calling. She was very good in the decorating department. Miss Patty had all those little "knick-knacks" as her mother labeled them and Miss Patty was happy for Amanda to do the arranging and it caught on to the point when Savage Media came to town, all the way from California, one thing led to another, they visited Miss Patty for items needed on the set of their documentary and that's where Clark entered the picture. Why wouldn't she jump to take a real job?

He was the director and after the documentary he was promoted to a higher position, better pay and on location near Asheville, North Carolina to do a documentary on one of the most prestigious old homes surrounded by acres of land that still grew cotton. Clark might be good at producing or directing a documentary but he didn't know one thing about a cotton farm. It did not meet his expectations nor did it bow to his will and Amanda being a farmer's daughter was asked to keep him notified of what was important in regard to that farm and more specifically, could she teach him the common terms associated with cotton farming? "I hear you are a cotton farmer's daughter," he said.

"Yeah." She pulled the suitcase from the back of the small SUV. After her parents' divorce, she had returned to work on the farm, but wouldn't enter her father's home. Sometimes there was a girl, around her age, with Bertha when she stopped by the fields. "Don't you know who that is?" One of the employees to the farm had been with her dad years longer than Amanda was old. "No, I don't," she'd replied. He had studied her with narrowed eyes before he yielded that information. "She's Bertha's daughter. Had 'er a year or so before she married your Pap. You want to meet her?" He didn't have to wait for that answer. "No." She did wonder if the girl used her room, slept in her bed? But she wouldn't ask Woodsey. Woodsey worried over her. He wanted what was best for her.

"You got any questions?" He watched her eyes take on a determined stare, her head raised as if facing an opponent, but it wasn't him. He heard the reply and forged ahead, "then I have one. Amanda, why don't you hang tight and one day take over as manager of Fair Acres?"

"Because," she'd said through thick lips, "Nothing's fair about that. He's got it set up as Fair, but I'm not allowed to hope one day I'll be in charge. If I had been a boy, he said it would've been different, but a woman can't face up to the struggle and challenge farming brings and he says it's only going to get worse as we go along." With that she walked away from Fair Acre's best employee, the one who taught her all those years, sometimes a hard task master seeing she got it right and other times a friend that backed her up when she met the challenge of the father that expect her to be a girly girl, as she called it. So here she was, on her way to more of the same with five years between. She closed the doors to the SUV if only she could close out the memories. She prayed Woodsey was still at the farm.

She noticed as she was wheeling in the suitcase, the office was piling up with people; a bus was moving away from the building as more people filed into the office. She made her way through the throng and headed down the hall. She heard voices coming from the manager's quarters; his, low and hers a cry full of unending pain. From the front, voices were calling down the hall. "We need help. You got rooms. Anyone here? We have reservations." Ignoring them, she went on down the hall.

Amanda knocked on the door. She heard him holler, "Not locked, come in." She opened the door to find him bending over his wife on the floor. "She fell again," he said. "Don't think any bones are broken but I'm trying to get her back on the bed and she can't help."

"Tell me what to do and I'll help."

"On the count of three, lift," he replied. She listened to him count and they lift at the same time.

"Sir, you have a room full of people down the hall. I'll stay with your wife while you check them in."

He wore such a pained expression she thought he was going to turn her down but almost as quickly that expression was replaced by tears pouring down his cheeks.

"Thank you, thank you. It wasn't always this way." He was straightening his clothing from the tussle he had been in trying to get his wife back on the bed. "Her name's Lois and," He took a deep breath, "She's dead weight. Don't know what I'm going to do." He turned toward the door. "Thank you. I'll hurry, best I can." He opened the door, pushed her suitcase inside and the door closed.

She prepared to leave the next morning and stopped by the desk to pay for the second night.

"I can't take your money," he said. "I would have been in a strait jacket yesterday if not for you."

"I'm glad I could help, Mr. Ferguson, but I want to pay." He wouldn't let her.

She went across the hall to tell Lois Ferguson good bye. "You won't see me again," Lois said, "But it's for the best because James can't keep this up and work, too." She held her arms out to Amanda. "May I hug you? You made a big difference for us, yesterday. Thank you, Amanda." She smiled,

"You are a blessing to your parents, I just know you are. Now be safe on your trip and I'll pray for you."

Memphis was as she remembered, high rise buildings, a housing project gone bad and the beautiful homes of the affluent. She passed the famous Children's Hospital. With the traffic sketchy she was coming to the convention center, where as a child, her parents took her with them the first of each year to attend the farm shows and view the newest farm equipment. Had she been a boy, her father would have trusted her to grow in to and take over the farm when he retired. He had seen the way she became involved; the men were willing to teach her but he couldn't see a girl capable of butting heads with the situations he did in order to keep the farm going. And here she was, on the North side viewing the Pyramid with all of its fame and history, really just a landmark belonging to Memphis. She entered one of the lanes of the Mississippi bridge with the muddy water churning below, crossing out of Tennessee and in to Missouri to take Interstate 55, heading North to where her father waited. No one knew she was coming unless her friend remembered and she preferred no one was there to make do over her when she had faltered once already. It was ironic he called, "Amanda, I need you. Will you come home?"

"Is there a reason you want me, now?"

"I'll tell you when you get here."

She had hung up the phone, sit down in the old brown chair and stared at the wall an hour or so. Their past was horrendous, how could she expect the future to be any better. They were the same individuals, or were they? It might be easier with Bertha gone but she just could not wrap her mind around that and yet, here she was driving home. The truth was she needed a place to stay. She had left North Carolina because of the embarrassment Clark created and she couldn't face the people of the small town. He was the famous one and she...she didn't want their pity. How had she come to this, that a man, whether it was Clark or her father had something to do with her life? Would she spend the rest of her life searching for Christmas?

Chapter 2

Tension was building, she felt nauseous at times. She had loved her father but then he betrayed not just her mother, leaving their marriage, he had left her, too. The impact had literally destroyed Amanda. Since she couldn't face her father with such rebellious thoughts, she told God it was his fault; he was supposed to be in charge, didn't she hear her parents ask him to protect her? It hadn't made sense, evidently it was out of their hands. She couldn't wait to grow up and be different.

She almost wanted to leave the route to her father's house and take her chances finding a job elsewhere and she meant somewhere away from the familiar people of her childhood and a life gone wrong. Hers. Thirty minutes off the Interstate and she was seeing farm land along both sides of the road, dormant and waiting for the first turn of the equipment to knock the tops off formed rows ready for planting. It was just as well she had been passed over but one thing was for sure, had her father chosen Bertha's daughter to the task she would never have returned to Fair Acres.

Two hours later she pulled in to the drive, everything looked the same. A light blanket of snow had covered the bayberry bushes on both sides of the house. She almost smiled remembering Phyllis saying, "I chose them because of the stickers, in an effort to keep you children from hiding under the house. You all thought it a great place to hide, I thought it a great place to be bitten by a snake."

Bertha probably didn't care. Uh, oh, watch the attitude girl. She pulled the main suitcase from the trunk, a show of positive intention that she was resigned to staying, come what may, at least a day. The walk up the red brick path her mother had laid, seemed a mile long. She knocked on the door and heard a faint "come in." Opening the door, she glanced around the room hoping to see him but he wasn't there. "In here," he called and she followed his voice to the dining room.

She felt the slight gasp of her own breath, "I did not know you are in a wheel chair, Dad."

"About a year now," he replied. "I thought you knew. Come sit, I need to present you with a serious proposition," and with that he began. When finished he sit back and waited for her reply.

"Am I understanding correctly, that you are offering to me a job that I would have willingly worked for you, freely, because I love you and I also wanted to learn, but you wouldn't allow it and now you would take me as an employee and I would be paid?"

"Yes." He sighed. "Years have passed, Mandy. I hoped you would have forgiven me by now, but you never said. Would you like to try your hand at running Fair Acres? As more than just an employee?"

"You never asked," she said, softly. "I thought you wanted to let things stand as they were."

"Pride," he said, "foolish pride. Will you take the job?"

"I am not current on anything to do with the farm, Dad. What I did in North Carolina was more as an Interpreter than anything. Clark, my boss, was a city guy...he had no idea about any of it." Her father was waiting. "Could I think this over, tonight, and get back to you tomorrow? And if I should take the position, who would I be dealing with, in regard to the current employees?"

"There is one new comer, with a bit more knowledge and desire to keep the others going, his name is Dante Rizzio. A little Italian in the blood explains the name, but you won't have any problems out of him. He worked on a farm in New York state before coming here."

"Is he qualified?"

"Definitely and keeps the others morale up." Suddenly he smiled. "Yours, too, if you let him."

"That scares me," she replied as they laughed together. "Something else, is the little house that belonged to grandmother still empty? It was, last time I was here."

"It is but you can stay here, if you wish. I'd be glad to have you for company. It's lonely here."

She smiled. "If I take the job, Dad, by the time someone repairs Grandmother Lanis little house, I have a feeling you will be happy to be rid of me." She stood up as she asked, "just in case, either way, how about I take up my suitcase and change into jeans and lets you and I take a drive in your truck around the operation and you can fill me in."

His face wreathed in smile. "I'd like that."

The afternoon had an unexpected twist. Charles suggested they drive by the farm shop. "It's changed a little," he said. She thought she read a bit of pride in the expression on his face. "Everyone will be home by now and we won't have to worry with introductions eating up the time." She nodded.

"And then there's supper," she said. "Does anyone see that you have a healthy diet?"

He grinned. "Your mother has a hand in that. Does she know you are back?"

"No, and I've been wondering how to explain to her why I'm staying here but her house is so small with the one bedroom and I want her to have her space without my being in the way."

"Can't she come over the evenings while you have decent hours? I know once field work begins will be a different story...' His voice trailed off as he glanced her way for confirmation. "Would that work?"

"You two are compatible now?"

He grimaced. "It was my fault, Mandy. I let a trollop that showed interest in the bedroom come between me and your mother and I nearly lost you to boot, in fact we both know I did for a while."

"Yes, you did, Dad. I never told you, one of your neighbors picked me up the evening I left here to walk home. He had a boy my age with him and I always wondered who he was. I saw him around school but he was quiet.

I think he might have been a year behind me and sometimes that makes a difference." She pulled close to the door. "Tell me what to do to get you out of the vehicle."

"I can walk a few feet. If you will check just inside that door, there's supposed to be a walker. If you will get it." From the glove compartment he brought out a chain of three keys. "Use this."

She thought she heard a noise in back of the shop. "Dad, is anyone supposed to be in here?"

"No, I don't think so, it's probably the air compressor coming on, it does that sometimes."

They were admiring a new piece of equipment when a man came around the corners floor to ceiling divider making a halt to his walk about the same time they did. Amanda went into a fighter mode; the man dropped what he was carrying and raised his hands as Charles started laughing. Immediately, Amanda let her hands drop.

"Well," she eyed the two men having a good laugh, at her expense. "I believe it's obvious you two know each other." Charles wiped the tears from his face, nodding his head all the while.

"Amanda, meet Dante Rizzio." Smiling, Charles explained, "Dan, this is my daughter, Amanda." Embarrassed and a little disconcerted at their laughter, she was aloof and found it hard to recapture the ease she and her father were previously enjoying.

If she hadn't been upset, possibly she would have found him charming. Perhaps thinking she had left intimidation behind and finding she had not, only time would clear the air between her and Mr. Rizzio. "I'll wait for you in the truck, Dad. Take all the time you need."

"Just a minute, Amanda, I was explaining to Dan that I won't be coming in from now on and I've asked him to help you get familiar to the changes we've made. I hope that meets your approval?"

"Sure. I've already noticed a few changes and it looks like it will benefit the company."

"To Dan's credit," Charles replied. "He's the one they look to and no one's disappointed."

The evening was ruined for Amanda. All she wanted was to go upstairs, crawl in bed and turn off the world. She had to be at the shop before any of the men in the morning and right now that was the last place she wanted to be. She stripped and stood in the shower, thankful for the release the warm water brought. She did not want to be anyone's boss. What she wanted was to fade into the woodwork and nurse her wounds.

She should have already called her mother, she did the least troublesome thing, sending a text. *"Mom, I'm here. I'm going to work at the farm. Tomorrow morning! I'll see you soon. Love you."* Mom would know her daughter's mood and wait for that promised call. Her mother promptly replied with two red hearts! Amanda felt such relief in her mother's love she cried.

If she slept that night, it was after wearing herself thin trying and when the alarm sound at six thirty, she wondered if she would be on time. The men appeared by seven. Dan asked them to line up and when they were settled, he introduced her. Woodsey winked, as in saying let's keep our relationship secret. She could have hugged him and knew she would when opportunity presented.

She worked the line, with a firm handshake and looking each one in the eye. They waited, expecting her to speak. She took a deep breath and began. "I grew up here and went on to college and in private business the last two years on a cotton farm in North Carolina. I can tell you that state ranks highly in production and the last report I received around Christmas there was over 1,037,000 bales produced last year and much of it will go into nearby mills. Have you ever wondered why our state can't do the same? Why are we working twice as hard and getting half the glory?"

"My father revealed you have been here through the thick and thin of his health issues and I want to thank you for that. His telling me, in case you don't know, is a huge admission that means you are highly valued. I may be a little rusty trying to remember how things are done here on Fair Acres. I hope you will grant me a period of grace and I'll do my best to grow in that grace."

"Very well said," Dante remarked as he led the way beyond the equipment where the men were working. "I assumed you would be interested in seeing your office." He opened the door into a very short hall some five feet deep, that led to a second door of sorts. He saw her staring. "It's a pocket door. You notice the book shelves on the walls? Well, your dad didn't want to waste an inch. He began this office for you around August, we'd work on it when it rained and the men got real interested in it as he told them he was gearing up to invite you back to run Fair Acres and you had to have a place to shine." He grinned, "yeah, those were his words. Here you go." He opened the door and motioned her in.

"Did you say my father began this office last August?" He nodded.

"Yes, Ma'am." She could tell he was waiting for something. She began to study each feature, the work spot, a computer, printer, a three-stack paper tray, a calculator, all you needed, and then she saw the square glass cannister filled with huge melt-in-the-mouth peppermint. Dante was nodding, as a smile widened to make his eyes light up. "That was so important to your dad. He had several stays in the hospital and on one occasion when things weren't looking so good, he said, "Now boys, you got to remember to keep my girl those fat peppermint candies. Individually wrapped, the puffy kind." Dante laughed, "I think we all came with a package the next Monday; it meant that much to him."

"When was this he was in the hospital?" She stood with one hand on the lid of the container. "That would've been just before Christmas. Your Mom came and stayed with him once he was released from the hospital."

"I never knew about that one." He seemed to understand her reluctance to ask more.

"I don't mean to intrude on your thoughts, Ma'am, but your daddy told me he made a terrible mistake in bringing another woman into the family and for a time lost you and your mother." He shuffled a bit before he added, "I find it a testimony to your parents that they have managed to form a friendship out of disappointment and care for each other after something that traumatic."

"I find it amazing, almost unbelievable," she said softly. "I lived through it and that is why I left."

"Both your parents are fine people…"

"You know my mother?"

"Sometimes your mother comes over and bakes and brings out good things for us to eat. Especially during someone's birthday."

"I can only wonder how that all happened…"

"The first time your daddy was ill and went to hospital, I drove him and when things didn't look good, he says, "Dan, will you go by my ex-wife's home and tell her what the doctor says and ask her to come with you tomorrow?" And I did, next day on my way," he paused, remembering, "and she cried when I told her and went in for her purse and rode to the hospital with me to see your daddy."

"That's my mother. Since you've met her, how many have been to church with her?"

Dan grinned. "I reckon we all have. I'm Catholic and I was probably the first to go with her."

Amanda gave him a disconcerting look, "I hate to ask, Dan, but has my father made you a manager or given you a title over the others?" She was beginning to think maybe Mr. Rizzio wasn't so bad.

"No, Ma'am, I didn't mean to cause you worry, I just told him I'd help out in any way to make your settling in easier." He seemed suddenly apprehensive. "I apologize for being too familiar…"

"It's not that, it's the fact my father put great store in your ability and he isn't wrong, you have good people skills and if the men follow your lead, then, we need to recognize it and I was thinking if you are good with the way things are, if you know what projects the men are working on and how they begin work each morning, then it will benefit everyone to continue and if I may ask a question, not because I would be questioning your work ethics or considering you trying to come in front of me, it seems they are all used to your way and I don't see reason to change it. How do you feel?"

Her first day of work, Amanda found the shop crew worked like a well-oiled machine. She had no idea what planting time would bring but for now they worked in the shop, not one run to tattle like some poor ignorant farm boy, instead they worked at a steady pace and she found time to find the farm ledgers and spend a few minutes studying each worker's back ground. It was six o'clock when the last vehicle left the farm shop and she closed the ledger. She had skipped lunch without noticing the hour slip by, but now she heard her stomach rumble as she walked to the car. She did not linger when she arrived back at her father's home.

Charles met her at the door "You stayed all day. Does this mean you accepted?"

"I believe I did." She grinned. "They are an interesting group, your farmhands."

"Ah, they are more than that." He could not hide his elation that she would be around. "When I first come down with this problem and was in the hospital, you'd thought I was dying the way they rallied."

"Why didn't you or Mom let me know?"

"What could you have done? I hadn't come to my sense yet, about our problem and your mom worked that one over me a good while. I was grateful she saw me through it."

"What is the problem?" They had progressed to the dining room and she sit at the table, ready to listen. "What has put you in the wheel chair?"

"There's a tumor, in my spine. I don't know if by now it's grown around it, but it started out right next to it and they ran all kind of scans. The long and short of it, the tumor has cut off whatever signal should go to the brain and allow me to walk, instead I'm in the chair and glad I can still get around."

"Are you in great pain? Can you walk at all? I mean as much as yesterday's distance."

He grinned. "Pain? Only when I move." He pointed toward the kitchen. "Ruby left food in the oven. Are you hungry? And if there's no other way, I try to walk, but it's a sad effort, you'll see."

"Starving." She started to rise. "Who is Ruby?"

"The house keeper, cook and bottle washer, all in one. And don't get any ideas, that's all."

Chapter

3

···

She knew Dante's knock. Tap. Tap. Tap.

"Come in." He stuck his head in. "Something wrong, Dan?"

"No, just the neighbor down the road farms next field over and he's been ditching after that last rain. Long story, short, his man on the tractor slid off in the ditch and he needs another to pull him out. You care if he borrows a tractor?"

"Shouldn't one of our men be the driver? I mean, it is an expensive piece of equipment."

Dan grinned. "Yes, Ma'am, but it's Jake and he is probably better on it than any of us. I mean, that fellow shoulda known not to get that close to the ditch but well, it happens."

"If this Jake is so good, where's his own tractor? I'm just trying to understand."

"Come out here and I'll introduce you to your neighbor. He's a few miles from his own headquarters and we are within a mile, less than a mile really…" He was waiting for her to come with him.

"Are you saying the guy on the tractor drove off into the big drainage ditch?"

"Yes, Ma'am and Jake, his boss, is out here waiting for permission to use our tractor."

"I'm hung up on the fellow in the big ditch. It's a wonder he wasn't hurt. Yeah, it's fine and I'll come meet our neighbor. You can make decisions like that, Dan." He was shaking his head.

"I think I'd rather not. That's why I came for you. In this case, though, he's young, the driver."

She followed him to the front of the shop. Out on the lot, a muddy pickup truck was being parked and a tall sandy haired man was getting out and walking their way. Once he stood within reach, Dan said, "Amanda, this is Jake Turner. He's our neighbor down the road."

Jake gave her a searching look as he offered a hand and she took it, but he didn't let go. "We kind of met, years ago. Glad to meet you again, Amanda Lanis."

"I don't recall. Did I know you in school or were you a grade ahead of me, that always seemed to make a difference." He paused for a minute as Dan was called away.

"Yeah, I might have been a grade or two ahead, but we met when my dad picked you up one night and drove you to your Momma's house."

That fateful night, Amanda was thinking, so he was the boy in the front seat of the truck.

"You didn't say a word." Her expression said it all. "I never knew your name."

"Well, you know it now." He grinned, still not turning loose of her hand. "I'm happy to meet you, Amanda. I'm told you are taking over here. So, Charles is going to turn loose. You think?"

She felt a bit insulted at the remark and tried to remove her hand. "Are you thinking I can't handle the job, Jake Turner?" There was challenge in her eye but regretfully a wistful tone to her voice.

"Can you handle.." Jake Turner saw something, but what? He stopped talking and kissed her.

Amanda sputtered free. "Hey, a stranger doesn't do....... that in broad daylight."

"But I'm no stranger," he corrected and she started to step away from him but not before he had thoroughly kissed her again and left her wondering where he'd been all her life, to which her mind reeled in the knowledge he had been "just down the road."

Laughing, he turned, hollering over his shoulder, "Thanks for loan of the tractor. I'll be calling you."

"What in the world does that mean?" She said the words out loud, turning to find Woodsey. "Did you see what he did, Woodsey?" Woodsey was shaking his head.

"Did he hurt you, Amanda?" Woodsey's expression was all concern. "Shall I go after him?"

"No, it wasn't that. I mean, what kind of person is he?" She was frustrated and puzzled.

Woodsey was relieved. "He's a fine person, Amanda, nose to the grindstone and all that. Jake went to college after school and as I understand had a good job, a good start at life but his dad got sick and Jake came home to help with the farm. The farm is in his hands now and he's doing well but I hear he works with a group of boys in his spare time, because of him they're a fine bunch makin' rank."

"Woodsey, take care of yourself. From what I'm hearing men wear out too soon. What is that about?" She saw sadness pass through Woodsey. "Tell me, what's going on in your life?" He was quiet. "I feel it, there was a dread came over you. Tell me. Come on, let's go in my office."

He followed but it was some time before he spoke. They just sit and looked at each other until he said, "Tina has cancer."

"Oh, no. This is just happening?"

"We found out last month, and she's on some kind of medicine and then they will be doing surgery."

"Breast cancer, Woodsey?" He nodded. "Do they know how far along it is?"

"I don't understand this stuff. Tina has talked to your mom. She's a little scared about being put to sleep."

"What do you need?"

"Nothing, except off that day, maybe a bit longer after the surgery." He stared at the floor a minute and then raised his head. Their eyes met. "The fellows, out there, don't know. Should I tell them?"

"What do you want to do? It's your call."

"I hate to tell them and you know we'll be planting by then and I'm one of the planter men."

"Is there one you think could take your place?"

"Not really, besides that, they've all got their own job to do." He was holding back on something.

"What is it?"

"My boy, Robert, he can fill my place if you let him. I've taught him. He's young and he hustles." He was studying the floor again. "I've been real careful teaching him." He sighed. "I hated to tell you."

She began to laugh. "Boy, the shoes on a different foot, isn't it. I used to hate to tell you." She rose out of the chair and leaned across to hug Woodsey. "Let's face that when the time gets here. Okay?" Woodsey was half way out the door when she thought of something. "Hey, did you say Robert?" She stretched her arm, hand-palm-down, "Did you say your little Robert knows how to run the planter?"

Woodsey stepped back into the office. "If you recall, he might have been that tall when you left for college but that's been, let's see...seven years?" A proud grin crossed Woodsey's face. "I'll bring him around."

"Something else, that Turner fellow, that borrowed a tractor, you said he was, your words, a fine person. Is he a stalker? He said he would see me again?"

Woodsey tried to hide his smile. "Amanda, give the boy a chance. You won't ever do better. By the way, we are shutting down early, like three o'clock this evening. Did your dad tell you? We've had a long week, with the ditching. Is that okay?" She nodded. "See you Monday, Amanda"

She sit at the desk. That was quite a statement coming from Woodsey, "you won't do better. Hmmm." She had no problem at all pulling his face back into memory. He smelled good, too, pretty far out for a farm boy. She wondered where he'd been so early to smell like that? But if he had a second business...it was a few minutes later she realized she had been day dreaming. It wasn't every day a complete stranger grabbed you and kissed you in broad daylight and you felt that kiss all the way to your toes. But he said he wasn't a stranger...Clark for all his made up gentleman ways couldn't hold a candle to.....she nipped that thought in the bud.

She made it through the morning and was well in to the afternoon when the ringing of the phone brought her around. "Fair Acre Farm," she answered, "Amanda speaking."

"Honey, it's Clark." She considered hanging up. "Babe. Babe. I know you are there." She slipped the phone on the cradle and heard it go silent but then he called back. She let the phone ring continually until she realized the men working in the shop could hear. She picked up the receiver.

"What do you want, Clark?"

"Oh, so you have the ability to change my name." She was stunned by an unrecognized male voice.

"How many times have you called this number?"

"Today," the caller replied, "one time, just now. I'm sorry but there's not enough magic in me to..."

"I apologize, Sir, but we've had a number of prank calls. How may I help you?"

"Well, seeing as I have your tractor and it's all muddy and I'm on my way to the car wash to clean it, I was thinking."

"Oh, it's you."

He didn't miss a lick, as he broke into song, "it's me.... I was wondering, do you suppose in one of those angel moments that all women seem to have, in one of those, is there any chance you could run me home once I'm back at your headquarters, seeing as how my man went home in my truck and then has signed out for the evening on a very important mission. My truck is there but no one to come pick me up as Terry had other stuff to do, important stuff..." he broke into song and she listened, shaking her head, the nerve. They had barely been introduced to each other. "What next?" She asked. She heard laughter and if she wasn't mistaken under his breath he said, "You want more?"

When she was quiet, he whispered, "I bet your men have clocked out, too. We don't have a clock. that's an idea, if you don't have plans for tonight, we could go look through those funny glass windows at the hospital and maybe see the new baby."

"You can't even whisper, my dad probably heard you inside the house."

"Ah, yes, man of the house. I wonder if he is enjoying his first days of retirement? Tell him I said hello, I like your father."

"Where is this car wash? You want me to pick you up there?"

"No, Ma'am. I will be back to your shop in about fifteen minutes and I will park this spanking clean tractor and then if you will drive me home,

I will forever be in your debt." She could hear the sound of running water. "Wowzah," he crooned, "I got a boot full then, turned the hose the wrong way. Be sure to tell your dad what you are doing so he won't worry."

"Yes, Sir," she said, "I can only imagine what the tractor looks like if you are washing it with a hose. I thought you said you are at a car wash. Wonders never cease."

"I heard that. I am at a car wash; I am handwashing the wheels."

⌒∞⌒

Hanging her jacket by the door, she had time to tell her father what she was doing.

"Dad, how well do you know the Turner guy that farms next to your land?"

"Jake?" Charles turned the volume down on the television. "Since he was a kid. You should know him. He lives down the road."

"Must be older than me, or younger. I don't remember him from school or the bus years."

"What about Jake?"

"He asked to borrow a tractor. Some kid was ditching, or so I was told and slid off in the ditch and since he was right here at your headquarters…"

"I'd trust Jake with anything, Hon. That kid, is probably Terry who is twenty years old."

"Well, it seems unusual to me but he asked if I'd drive him home, the kid drove his truck home and didn't return, his wife's having a baby and he's at the hospital."

"Must be Terry's wife. Everyone knows each other's business." He gave her a searching glance, "Is there more to this story?"

She shrugged. "Like what?" They were interrupted by someone at the door, knocking in an unusual way. She opened it to find her mother, with a cooler in one hand and a covered casserole in the other.

"What in the world are you doing?"

"Didn't he tell you? I'm early and I brought supper." She gave Charles a scathing look. "Not that tubby there needs it. I declare, Charles, have you sat there all afternoon?"

"It's early yet. What can I do? Did you know Vanna White is leaving the show"

"No, that's not right. She may have taken a day or two off because her father died."

Amanda watched them. They turned to listen to her opinion. "You two," she said, shaking her head. "I'll put the food in the kitchen, or do you want it on the dining room table?"

She heard the knock at the door and her mother say, "Jake, what a nice surprise, come in here."

"Can't Miss Phyllis, I had a little run in with a water hose and my pant leg is wet."

Charles voice boomed out, "step in here, Jake, and let me see you. Lord knows water won't hurt." By that time, Phyllis had hold of his hand, bringing him in to the room. "What's this about you on foot?" Phyllis gave Jake a glance and then Charles. "I think he's stranded. Was it Terry's wife had a baby?"

Jake was nodding as Amanda came back into the room. She had dashed upstairs and changed into a pair of jeans and a loose white sweater. "If you're going to be out better take a jacket,' her mother cautioned, "this weather we've been having has been unseasonal."

"Mother, I'm just driving Jake home." To Jake she said, "I'm embarrassed, just ignore my folks."

"Well, you couldn't find a nicer young man."

"Mother."

"I second that," Charles agreed.

"Now the two of you get along." Amanda threw her hands up in the air. "I give up."

"Don't worry Miss Phyllis, Charles, I'll take good care of your daughter and if you all don't care, I'll even feed her, if she will stay." He sent Amanda a pleading glance, "I don't bite, truth is I haven't eaten lunch. And we could go see the new baby. That would tickle Terry."

"So, Amy Lou had her baby," Phyllis smile landed on Amanda.

"Let's get out of here," Amanda felt the need to escape. "I can only imagine what comes next."

Jake left laughing. "You all have a good evening."

"If she gets balky," Charles called, "You all just come back here and we'll all eat together."

"Fresh lime pie," Phyllis added. "Food's ready, I came early to visit, guess I'm stuck with Charles."

"Can you believe that?' Amanda heaved a heavy breath, "As my dad says, a bar maid and a number of years later they get along better than ever but they live in two separate houses."

"Has he asked her to come back?" Amanda nodded. "Enough said, let's talk about something else." He suggest, "How about barbeque? I bought some this morning when we had our annual Boy Scout fund raiser. Miss Gloria packed up the whole kit and caboodle and said she'd deliver it later."

They rode most of the way to his house in a comfortable silence, and that mystified Amanda, usually she felt either nervous or intimidated by a new male, whether working or socializing but Jake for all the previous teasing and silliness was comfortable to be with.

"I know you live down this road, but I don't recall where."

"You can't miss it, there's a small excavator blocking the entrance, in preparation for tearing out the remaining concrete and putting in a new drive, but first things first."

"Meaning?"

"There has to be a new culvert and I did have one ordered but some monkey delivered the wrong one and there's no way it's large enough. You can bet that guy lost his job. You'll see, there's a great difference in what's needed and what was delivered."

"So, do I drive in or park on the side of the road." She now had the excavator in sight.

"I think if you will take the second drive, you can pull right up within feet of the back door, if you don't mind a back door entrance." She did as he instructed and followed a strip of gray rock through green lawn, a picnic table with a bright blue umbrella and a white gazebo equipped with four lawn chairs.

"Nice, did you do this?"

"Yeah, I did. I have the Scouts out here on occasion and we needed some order. The gazebo is large enough I can take the chairs out and they usually sit on the ground or some piece they bring. They aren't sissies, meaning no offense." he grinned, "Something tells me you're no sissy either."

"Really, what gives you that impression?"

"I don't know, maybe because your dad chose you over Dante to take his place managing the farm."

"You know Dante well?' She dropped the keys into her jean pocket and followed him to the door.

"After you, my lady." He was stripping as he walked, boots, shirt, cap, filling the cap with keys, a small screwdriver and a lot of loose change. "don't worry, I'm stopping there but I will run in and get a shower if you can entertain yourself just, say, fifteen minutes…I've got a lot of grime on me."

She was getting her bearings when he said, "straight ahead, on the left the living room and on your right my favorite spot, you'll see." That piqued her interest.

"I'll take the door on the right."

"I thought you would." He was hurrying down the hall. It wasn't a second until she heard running water.

She guessed it was his man cave, but she felt comfortable in it. On one wall three guitars and a banjo were the focal point; beneath them a baby grand piano and that surprised her. She had taken lessons and though she aspired to own a baby grand all Charles could come up with was an old upright he purchased when the five and dime movie theatre went out of business. It was pretty well worn by the time she got it but he stuck to his guns in saying, "we need a new piece of farming equipment not a piano for you to bang on." In her vicious moods she had wondered if Bertha's daughter played the piano and she didn't know if she was mad or glad the girl didn't and the old piano appeared untouched.

There didn't seem to be sheet music available. She settled on the bench anyway and ran a few scales before she launched into Moon River and was pretty well engrossed in the resonance of the instrument as she played the theme song from Peyton Place when he came in and set beside her on the bench, picking up the rendition she had heard a million times.

"We were just kids when our mother's watched that program and while I don't remember much of the dialogue I remember the theme song," he said, "and I couldn't wait for the program to finish so I could hit the piano and give it my all."

She laughed, "I know but I was playing on an old upright Dad bargained for when the old theatre went out. Like the theatre, it last beyond it's time. How did you rate a baby grand?"

"I didn't. Last year a friend was ready to hock this one. He hit a really bad time, lost his business and was moving away, as he said for greener pastures and he needed money to move. I helped him and he gave me the piano when it wouldn't fit properly in the cargo trailer and it was probably just as well, he hit a curve too fast and upended the trailer and lost everything. But not to worry, he moved in with his girlfriend and they're married now."

"Why aren't you married?" She rose from the bench, giving him more room. "Play something for me." She watched while he ran the keys, a classical that end in a barrelhouse oldie.

"Boogie Woogie at its best," he said. "To answer your question, I am not married because I haven't found anyone that would put up with me. And right now, let's eat!" With that, he led to the kitchen, brought out a basket, "Delivered an hour ago, according to Miss Grace, and ready to eat."

"They have access to your home? You must trust them."

"I do. They are the seventy-eighties group and I love them." He gave her a cloth napkin.

"You are quite a Casanova, aren't you?"

"Aww, should my feelings be hurt? On what, may I ask, do you base that statement?"

She spread the napkin in her lap, "delicate as this subject might be, I will approach it. You are the first man that kissed me in the midst of our being introduced."

"Twice, I believe." He gave her a most beguiling smile. "That was a first for me. You looked like you needed kissing." Suddenly he was very sincere. "I felt this magnetism, drawn to you. I kissed you the second time to see if you felt it, too." He was waiting for her reply. A very long minute passed. "Aww, come on, tell me. I won't eat another bite until you tell me... something...anything."

"Give me a bit of time to know you, who you are, and then I'll tell you."

Her phone buzzed and she stopped it without a glance to see who was calling. She was listening to Jake. She dare not tell him the kiss left an impression, he would pursue the issue full length. "We could practice, during your time of deciding." He registered the look she gave him. "Or, not." For a time, he settled down to eat and they enjoyed a regular conversation. By six thirty they had cleared the table, hand washed the dishes and in all had a good evening even if her phone buzzed repeatedly. He said, "You can take your calls, if you wish, it doesn't bother me."

"Maybe I should go and I'll see who is calling on my way home."

He glanced at the clock, "it's early yet and we haven't checked in on the new baby, either."

"That's right, your friend. You have been a great host and I appreciate the charm of your home."

"Thanks for driving me," he said. "Will you be settling in with one of your parents?"

"Actually, if Grandmother's house can be salvaged, I have plans to live there."

"Mrs. Lanis left it in pretty good shape and she's not been gone that long."

"I hope there's no major problems. So, thanks for the dinner."

"I'll walk you to your car." The phone buzzed again as he held the door. "I think you have a boyfriend trying to find you. Does this mean I have some pretty important competition?"

She laughed. "If there was a boyfriend, would I have left North Carolina?"

"My first sign of encouragement. Thank you." He shut the door and did a high jump.

She drove out the gravel path shaking her head. "Who are you?" She was laughing until her phone rang again.

"Amanda, don't hang up. I need you to listen. I'm coming near your area and I want to see you."

"There's no need, Clark. We have nothing to say to each other." She closed her phone, but it rang before she could lay it on the console. "I mean it, I have nothing to say to you."

"Amanda, it's Jake." The tone of his voice got her attention.

"What's wrong?"

"I know you just left but I was wondering, would you go with me to the hospital?"

"I'm puzzled, your voice sounds different."

"I know. I've just had terrible news. It can't get any worse."

"I'm just pulling in to Dad's, come by and pick me up."

"I'm half way there."

She ran in to find her mother still with Charles. They were sitting across from each other talking in hushed voices. She felt something had happened. Why else would they look so sad.

"The young woman who had the baby," Phyllis began, "had a blood clot and died. Terry was so upset he left the hospital and no one knows where he's going."

"Who told you?"

"One of the nurses is part of our church prayer chain," Phyllis replied. "She called and we are trying to figure out how to handle letting the others know without intruding on Terry in any way."

"Jake is picking me up to go with him to the hospital. What do I do? I don't know Terry."

"Jake knows him. They're friends. It will be all right. You will be there for Jake's support." Phyllis rose up to kiss her daughter's cheek. "Be safe." Amanda felt the need to kiss both of her parents and was down the steps as Jake pulled into the drive.

"Terry's wife has died," Jake said, as she got in the truck. "She's everything to Terry. I'm worried he will go off the deep end."

"He left. My mother received a call from one of the Nurses who is part of the church prayer chain."

"Oh, me." He pound the steering wheel. "What I was afraid of, he won't remember the baby, he will drive and end up somewhere we can't find him."

"Who called you?"

"Probably the same nurse. I attend the same church. She said Terry gave her my name and ask if I would come. I was already in the truck, when I got the call. Since you left early, I thought I'd go in and see the infant and offer congratulations. I had no way of knowing this..."

"Does Terry have someone to help with the baby? I mean, a newborn… think about it."

"That's the thing, Terry and Amy Lou met through a rehabilitation program, or something like that, and they neither have family, their history is beyond believing to regular run-of-the-mil folks, but that's what brought them together and its been a strong tie. I got the kids interested in church and what can I say…they were excited to have this baby, said they were going to have a strong family finding each other as they did."

"Now she's gone…"

Jake gave her a sad glance, "And we don't know where he is; his world has crashed around him." Taking the phone from his pocket, he tried to reach Terry. "I know he has his phone but he won't answer."

They were another fifteen minutes arriving at the hospital. Jake made a pass through each lane looking for Terry's pickup. "Man, I prayed it would be parked in one of these spots and we'd pull him out whole bodied and not layin' dead behind the wheel."

"You're worried he will do something drastic?" Jake nodded. Amanda felt fear clutch her heart. "Come on," he said, "Let's go in to the hospital on the chance he has returned to his child."

"Do you know if the baby is a boy or a girl and is it stable?"

For a moment, Jake had a bewildered look on his face. "I didn't think to ask, I was so worried over Terry but I assumed he was there with the baby."

"Evidently my mother felt the same, or she would have told me." He opened the door and they entered the hospital. "Do you know where we are going?" A nurse was coming toward them. Amanda heard Jake say, "Thank God."

"I've been waiting for you. Follow me." Amanda fell in step, thinking this must be the Nurse. "Amy Lou is still in the room and Terry can't be found. Out of respect, someone that knows them needs to be present, don't you think? Terry put you down as next of kin."

"What about the baby?" Jake seemed almost petrified. "Is it all right?"

"It is a she. She is fine and they named her even before she was born. Abigail Christine, the Christine as I understand is after your mom. Did Terry and Amy Lou know your mother?"

"Yeah, they did," he replied in an almost tone of disbelief. "I can't believe this is happening."

"For what it's worth, I guess because I knew them, neither can I." She led to the elevator and punched the button to second floor, and when it stopped, she led them to a room just around the corner from the nurses' station.

Amanda would forever remember the bed sheets were so white they were startling but then again it may have been because Amy Lou's dark hair fanned out on the pillow and her color was not the pale of one who had died. She appeared to be in a restful sleep, her arms uncovered but to her side. The nurse pat Jake's hand as she said, "Hospital personnel may try to run you out. Tell them to see me."

"What about the baby? I know I asked but what's going to happen to the baby?"

She gave him a worried look. "I'll have to let administration explain that to you." She seemed to have a second thought. "Would you like for the baby to be brought in? It's important, anyway we on this floor think it's important a new borne be held within a certain time by someone who is family."

Amanda realized the nurse eyes rest on her after that and then as if propelled by an inner force she was hurrying out the room. Surely not, Amanda was thinking and she put the thought aside.

They heard the siren as through the window they saw an ambulance enter the hospital drive for ER.

"Please, God," Jake whispered. "Don't let that be bringing Terry in," and he stepped to the bed as if to comfort Amy Lou. "It feels almost sacrireligious, our being here and not her husband."

He sounded so distraught, Amanda reached out to hold his hand as Jake's eyes closed, and somehow, she knew he was praying Terry was safe.

Once the door opened, and closed as footsteps sound down the hall and then it opened again as a clear bassinet of sorts was wheeled into the room to reveal a tiny little replica of Amy Lou wrapped in a blanket imprinted with tiny pink bows and wearing a pink knit cap that did not cover all of her hair.

Amanda heard a wistful awestruck voice say, "Oh, she's beautiful. Look at that dark hair." Too late she realized she had spoken but the nurse just nodded and smiled as she turned to leave the room.

As the minute hand of the clock on the wall made its round, Jake's composure seemed to be slipping and intensified when the Nurse that accompanied them to Amy Lou's room returned and ask, "Jake are you up to holding little Abigail?"

He swallowed almost near tears. "Amanda will hold her, if that's all right with you." He gave her a beseeching look as he took a deep breath. "I don't think I'll be at ease until Terry is standing by my side." As an afterthought he explained, "Lindsey and I attend the same church. Lindsey, this is Amanda Lanis, Charles and Phyllis's daughter."

The nurse pat his arm again and turning to Amanda, said, "I know your parents. We all attend Hope Central. Now, let's get a gown over your clothes. But first wash your hands over there, really good."

"Should I fill out some kind of form or something that I've not been sick in the last so many days?"

"Have you?" Amanda shook her head, no. "Have you been out of country? I'll get the necessary papers and you can sign them but if you and Jake are friends..." She paused as there was a knock at the door, stepping out she returned with a second nurse, saying, "This is Sammie Kay, she will stay in here while you hold little Abigail. Jake, come with me, and we'll get those forms."

"Is it all right to hold the baby in Amy's room?" Amanda was fighting a battle of her own.

"If it was you, what would you want?" Amanda stared at the nurse as she whispered, "yes."

She wasn't sure, because so much was happening too fast, but Amanda knew she would never be the same. If she could have taken little Abigail home, she would not have hesitated, not even a minute. She was no bigger than her last doll of Christmas nearly twenty years past, but the yawning and grunting were sounds that spoke to her heart as Abigail accepted being on the outside of her mother's womb breathing on her own instead of a steady flow of oxygen provided by her mother. The squirming only emphasized more, here was a miracle of God's love bestowed on parents that looked forward to her birth and all the years to come, except the mother had left this earth. Amanda wondered what would happen to this child. Fifteen minutes passed quickly and as the nurse took the baby, Amanda told Amy Lou good bye and what a fine baby she had given life to, that she would be praying the child's life would be blessed with a good mother someday when Terry was ready. And as she settled in the downstairs waiting area of the hospital, she was filled with wonder that her arms felt empty having held the baby so short a time.

Jake's energy engulfed her as he found her and said, "We can leave." It was obvious something had not gone as expected but since they had only known each other a day, though it seemed an eternity, she would not ask but if he wanted to tell her what he was feeling she would listen. He did not immediately leave the parking lot, but leaned forward almost draping himself over the steering wheel. "Do you have time, if we drive over to the Old Park Pond?" She nodded and he put the truck in gear.

Once they were parked, on the patch of gravel that separated the city street and the pond, with the moonlight gleaming on the water's surface, he turned to her, struggling to form the words, until at last he said, "I had this heavy feeling when that ambulance turned into the hospital drive that something was terribly wrong. A vision of Terry washed through my mind and I shuddered inside in fear something would happen to him." His voice was husky with emotion. "Terry would do anything for me. As I would him. We were more than employer and employee. I have watched him grow into being a man, a husband to Amy Lou, but most of all a helper willing to go the second mile and smart, too. Together we figure out how to make things better."

"Is he hurt?" The same fear she felt hours earlier was battering her mind.

"He's dead. It was Terry in that ambulance. He wrapped his truck around a tree and they think he died instantly." With those words he placed his forehead against the steering wheel and stared at the post below. "I can't believe all this has happened since we went to the field together this morning."

"Oh, it's ..." She was at a loss for words. Compassion rose up to choke her saying more. "That sweet little baby." Tears ran down her cheeks.

"Do you mind if I ask...I mean, I know I'm being selfish asking, but I just don't know how this happened all in one day and I haven't been able to fully wrap my mind around it yet." He wiped a hand across his face as if to rid the horror of death taking two people, young people, he knew. "Could we go back to my house and play the piano together or talk...I don't know what to say..."

"Let me call my dad and explain I'll be late. Better still, I'll just text him."

"Wouldn't it be nice to be out on the water, in a boat, drifting along, no cares in the world?"

"If it were summer," she replied, and they laughed together, their voices making a husky sound.

Charles replied to her text that she had a key. Her mother had left and he would be asleep.

He drove a slower speed, taking the same back drive she'd taken earlier and this time he unlocked the back door to let them in. "Are you hungry," he asked and when she shook her head, he said, "Me neither. My Mom always said she could tell when I was trying to work through something because I'd sit and play the piano for hours. I did and when I thought it through, I usually had a plan."

She took the arm chair next to the piano. "I'll listen." For some reason he began with hymns and by the time he reached The Old Rugged Cross, the humming he began manifest to singing the words. It was then she sit beside him, her hand on his back. They did not sing loudly, but together as though meditating; words that brought comfort. Finished, he stood, took her hand and led her to the sofa. But he did not sit. He stood, holding her hand, looking at her with a sad expression.

"May I hold you? I won't get out of line. I promise." He tried to smile. "My Dad died three years ago and then Mom last May, almost a year, liking two months and I thought I was gaining ground. I'm a big old guy...and I've dated, but I've not been involved. There's just something about another person's touch, you...you know?"

"I know," her voice was barely audible. Her private thoughts would not bare the secrets of her heart. Her story was too raw, she kept thinking in time...perhaps in time she could share but not yet.

He drew her to his body, his lips against her hair and she felt the tears sliding down her neck into her sweater as his hold tightened. He could not know; she had thirst for another's touch but she had been rejected. Once she prayed God would change him and then for a good man that cared to replace the one who scorned her, but her faith was dim, even knowing she must put him aside. He was not worth the hurt that ran so deep she had come home, lest she fall back into his arms knowing he would never value her but would use her and think nothing of it. Hadn't he laughed and said women were a dime a dozen and a man of his caliber deserved much more? Why, she had asked. You don't realize who I am, he replied, I'm expected to have the best. I deserve it," Clark had said. She felt Jake's grief take hold; his body was shaking and she pulled him down on to the sofa where they sit for hours.

He dropped her off at her dads after midnight. "I have to go back to the hospital tomorrow evening. Do you want to keep me company?"

"What about funeral arrangements? You said neither Amy Lou or Terry had family. I can't imagine."

"Nor I," he agreed. "I know they had some kind of plan but I don't know how much. I don't even know if anyone could get that information. Shall I pick you up around five tomorrow evening?"

She nodded. "If that's what you want. Since I didn't know Amy Lou or Terry, I don't want to intrude."

"You know me," he said. "Listen, I'm sorry about my emotional breakdown, big boys aren't supposed to cry."

"No?" She smiled, "But when real men cry it shows they care about others. See you tomorrow." He waited until she was inside and smiled, as he was leaving.

She washed her face and crawled into bed. She would shower in the morning. She almost forgot she had turned off her phone and glanced at it before turning out the light. Clark had loaded her text and filled the voicemail. She edited, clearing both. Ordinarily, she would have read each one and listened just to hear Clark's voice. He was bluffing when he said he was coming to this area.

❧

The next morning as she was stepping out of the shower, her phone was ringing.

"Amanda, did Terry show up? I can't help thinking about that little baby."

"Mom, you haven't heard? Terry died last night. Wrapped his truck around a tree."

"Oh, my, our Father in heaven," Phyllis concern came through. "Oh, my, what about the baby?"

"Stable and beautiful, Mom, but I can't talk or I'll be late for work, could you tell Dad?"

By the time she arrived, the men were in a huddle talking about Terry and Amy dying. "What do you make of this?" Woodsey ask. "Someone called Tina this morning. She cried something terrible."

Amanda escaped the questions. "I'm new here. Remember?" The men began work in a somber mood. It seemed work kept their minds busy but they were ready to clock out when quitting time arrived and hurry home to family. She overheard one say, "we don't know whether we'll see our loved ones the next day or the next hour, do we?" She placed her phone in the desk drawer. She didn't want to have to answer if Clark started calling as he had when she was at Jake's house.

She had dressed, to leave from work, to go with Jake to the hospital. He was on time. "My men couldn't concentrate on work; I told them to go home early. Truth is, I couldn't either."

Lindsey was leaving as they entered the building. "Hey." She was trying to read how Jake was handling the situation. "Amanda, they are waiting for you upstairs to hold the baby. They have their hands full, must be a full moon, word says there's three momma's-to-be in labor and on their way in."

Amanda sensed Jake wanted to say something. "I was hoping you would sit in on the meeting with me and then we can go up together to see the baby."

"Works for me, but don't you think we need to start calling Abigail by name so she won't grow up thinking her name is baby?"

"But if she goes through adoption, the new family might want to rename her."

"Adoption?" Amanda's countenance dropped. "That makes my heart ache. I hadn't thought of adoption."

"Amy Lou and Terry would want the best for their little...baby...Abigal or my preference, Abby."

"Oh..."

"You look like you are going to cry. Please don't cry, yesterday just wiped me out and I might start all over again and it won't look manly in front of the administrator." He put a finger under her chin. "There, buck up. We can do this...together." He knocked and a male voice bid them enter.

"Jake." He waited for an introduction. "This is confidential business, for the sake of Terry and Amy Lou's little girl, and all the "hoopla" that's bound to surface in regards to her parent's dying. I say confidential and hoopla, because you wouldn't believe the calls I'm getting as far away as Canada."

"In what regard?" Worry lines creased Jake's brow. "How would they know."

The administrator pointed to the computer. "You've heard of internet, TikTok?"

"I can leave," Amanda said politely.

"No, No, No." He held out a hand. "I'm Jeff. This big buffoon and I went to school together."

"One buffoon to another," Jake said, "Meet Amanda Lanis. Phyllis and Charles's daughter."

"Love your mother; she makes the best apple pie ever."

"What did you mean, hoopla?" Jake wore the worried look again.

"Wanting to adopt the child but I tell them it's all taken care of."

"How's that?" Jake had taken the first chair and was settling in for Jeff's story.

"The papers are all in order and she can go home today."

Jake stood, his chair making a slapping sound on the tile. "Who decided? I mean, someone needs to be sure the right person has Terry and Amy Lou's little girl. I'm truly upset, Jeff. Not just any Tom, Dick or Sherry can take their child without a board meeting to decide the right person has been chosen."

Jeff eyed Jake in complete and total disbelief. "But Terry and Amy decided, Jake. A month ago."

Jake leaned in, his hands palm down on Jeff's desk. "They're dead, Jeff. What are you trying to pull?"

Jeff met him head on, nose to nose. "There you go, Turner, jumping to conclusions. Now, I suggest you sit back down. For once, you can't ramrod this situation, well, maybe you can, but don't. Hear me out. There's always papers to sign these days on any hospital stay and when the two saw the questions they took them quite seriously. Serious enough they saw a lawyer, drew up a will and something akin to adoption papers, saying in the event something happened to either of them, which they were sure it wouldn't, but anyway, if it did, the future of their child would not be left hanging as theirs were."

"Okay, so I'm calm now." Jake glanced quickly to Amanda. "Sorry. Sorry. I'm still a bit uptight."

"Yeah, matters of the heart makes him…well, let's just say I know him." He turned full attention to Jake. "You do remember, Terry list you as next of kin?" Jake nodded. "Would it surprise you to know you can take little Abigail home with you tonight?" Jeff sighed. "The hospital sends home a week's supply of diapers, formula, a number of blankets, gowns and other essential items a baby requires, all donated by the ladies auxiliary and very helpful until a shopping trip can be managed if there's no layette waiting."

"Why in heaven's name would I take the little one home with me if they had everything arranged? As usual, you don't make a lick of sense."

"You know what, dumbo? Our facility is full to the stretching point. It's been a long day, I'm tired, I'm hungry and my wife is waiting. You should get yourself one of them, if you could get along with one."

"I'm trying here, Jeff. Sorry I irritate you. My best friend and his wife have both died leaving a helpless infant that I promised to be part of that child's life if it were possible and didn't infringe on anyone else. So, now that I'm sitting reasonably sensible and sane why don't you tell me who you have given their child to, so at this point I can retrieve my friends baby girl."

Jeff appeared confused. "Before I gnaw my fingers to the bone, tell me, Jake, didn't Terry discuss any of this with you, or for that matter, Amy?

Jake hung his head, tears rolling down his cheek. "I give up. We did discuss it and he said there was only one person he would trust his family with, that meant Amy and the baby if anything happened to him. I feel completely ashamed that I wouldn't cross that barrier and ask who, because I see now, I should have but I was trying to be a decent friend and give him privacy and not try to influence his and Amy's decision." He arose. "Listen, we've been friends since first grade. I'm sorry. I loved Terry. He was a friend, just like you are and I apologize to you too." He turned toward the door. "Let's go, Amanda."

"Hey, Buddy, I know you are hurting. That's the kind of guy you are. Go on up and see little Abigail. They should have her ready for you." Jeff came from behind the desk. "Nice to meet you, Amanda. Maybe the four of us could get together sometime and Bud, don't forget to take the baby home with you tonight."

Jake's hand was on the door handle. "I still don't think that's the best idea, Jeff."

"She's yours, Jake," Jeff said softly. "Terry and Amy signed papers at the attorney's office. It's all legal and she's yours." Jake was going out, nothing seemed to register and then suddenly he turned. "That's right, Jake. They didn't know what was going to happen but if it did, they left her to you."

"You will need to get a larger car seat," the nurse was saying as she made adjustments to the straps. "It is against the law to travel with an infant, other than in a car seat, and this is for the first months. You can return it when you find your own and the same goes for the Bassinett. We always try to keep a couple on hand and we do clean them for the next baby because sometimes folks aren't prepared."

She stepped away from the truck. "Good thing you have that rear seat in your truck. Now we wish you the best of luck and we're sorry about the circumstance. I'm not from here but I did hear people saying what a sweet couple the parents were. They said the funeral arrangements are on hold?"

"Yeah, they are." Jake gave Amanda a knowing glance and when they were down the road, he said, "If I thought I was in shock before, there's no word for how I feel now."

"I have a bit of that surprise dashing through my veins, too." Amanda turned to study the sleeping baby. "What will you do, hire a sitter?"

"How does one go about finding a person you trust with a new born baby?" In the dark of the cab, he rolled his eyes. "How am I to finalize funeral arrangements for this baby's parents, tomorrow and take care of her, too?" Almost, he chuckled. "Do you find out of the sadness of this situation, there's something so ironic it's almost funny?"

"What's that?"

"Yesterday I snotted all over your hair, with my unmanly crying crocodile tears over Terry and Amy Lou and today, maybe, just maybe I should be crying over this unexpected situation. Instead, I have the urge to throw my head back and laugh like a lunatic. I think the world has gone crazy or I have one."

She sit there trying to figure out a way to help him but she was a single woman, he was a single male and she had a job she had to attend to. "I can help you tonight," she said. "Since you have all the paraphernalia it appears a baby needs." She took out her phone and text her dad. It was only seconds after she sent the text, her phone rang. "It's dad," she said, but it wasn't.

Phyllis voice came over the line, actually her laughter. "I find this almost hilarious. But I am trying to sober up. Sober as not laughing at your situation. I brought dinner again, thinking I'd see you, but you are out galivanting around with our most eligible bachelor."

"It's not like that, Mother. I wish I hadn't put my phone on speaker.'

"You sound tired, dear. Does Jake, by any chance need a baby sitter? I could help out and if it proves to be acceptable to everyone, baby included, we might help in raising this little girl."

Jake spoke up. "Miss Phyllis, you are the answer to prayers I just started praying a couple hours ago. There was no way I could have believed a baby girl was going home with me tonight. But I start out early in the mornings, are you sure you could handle those hours?"

"If it gets to me, do you have a second bedroom you're not using? I might have to stay over. Not to inconvenience you, but seriously if you start early and work late, we would need plan B, don't you think?"

"How do we do this? Do we take the baby in first or the stuff?"

Jake was showing signs of stressing out again; she was learning to read him. "How about I take Abigail in and you start unloading the baby things to inside the back door and then we will put them away together." She retrieved Abigail from the car seat and slung the diaper bag over her shoulder. "Hey, we probably were supposed to take Abby in the car seat, you think?"

"I can run a farm but I don't know a thing about a baby."

"It's okay, we will learn together."

"Promise? You won't jump ship?" She was shaking her head, Abigail in her arms. "I'd marry you on the spot if you'd say yes." He lingered, a pitiful expression on his face. "I need a wife."

"You don't know me. I might be Harriet the hatchet woman. "If you think you can't handle a baby you don't need me. Now go get the bassinet." He seemed at a loss to the meaning of the word. "The little hooded bed. Kind of small on folding legs, remember?"

"Right. Folding legs. To hood or not to hood. Right? I thought it was a stroller."

"No, you have to buy that. Do you not have any nieces or nephews?"

"I'm an only child. Remember? I told you. Didn't I?"

"No, I didn't know you. We didn't ride the bus together, did we?"

"My mother drove. She was a teacher."

"Ah, that explains a few things. Now, the box with sheets, blankets, gowns. It's a big box in the back of your truck." She saw the light dawn in his eyes. "Yeah, that one. You're getting it now."

"Did we eat? I don't remember eating. Wasn't I going to feed you?"

"It doesn't matter. More important things came up. I think this one needs feeding. She's searching." Amanda studied the baby in her arms. "I have never held a baby this long. She's beginning to feel like she belongs. She kind of molds to your body. You'll see. Amanda motioned with one finger, "Come look, see how she's moving her mouth and hear that little sound?" She smiled. He was in awe of this little bundle in her arms. "Could you run a big cup of almost hot water and set the bottle of formula in it. That's the old-fashioned way, so the nurse said, but a good way to warm the milk." She watched him, as she gave Abigail gentle reassuring pats on the bottom.

"Now press just enough I can feel it on my wrist. Yeah, that's good. Try it on your wrist before I give her the bottle."

"What if I burn her, I might get it too hot." He tried. "It's barely warm, but what if I…"

"That's why you test it." She settled into the only kitchen chair that had arms. He watched in amazement as the little girl, now three days old began to accept the bottle's nipple and then slowly she began to draw the milk. Their eyes met; he felt an incredible contentment he'd not experienced before as though he had something to do with her achievement. "Isn't she something."

He successfully applied the pad and then the sheet over the bassinets small firm mattress and she lay the baby burped and diapered down to sleep and wrapped her snug in the light weight blanket. "The nurse said for a week or so to wrap the blanket just enough that she would feel secure, kind of a replica of when she was in her mother's womb." He was shaking his head. "What?"

"How do I remember all this stuff? Do I write it down?" His attention turned to the stack of boxes. "What's next?" His stomach rumbled and he glanced to see if she heard. He thought not.

She was eyeing a small chest by the door, prior to entering the hall to another room. "Is that your bedroom?" He nodded. "Is there anything special in this chest of drawers?" She had her hand on it. He opened a drawer that revealed a few skeins of yarn. The second and third were empty. "That's unusual to find empty drawers," she said. "Women are known for using empty space."

"One of the women at church mentioned she sewed and I gave her mother's stash of quilt scraps, you know, those small squares of different colored material women use for quilting."

"No, I don't know a thing about sewing, except maybe sewing on button or hemming trousers."

He grinned. "I was beginning to think you know everything." He removed the yarn. "So, what are we doing? Putting her clothes in the drawer? If so, let me get a damp cloth and wipe them out."

"Well," he stood back satisfied with the look of Abby's clothes, meager stack as they were, on the shelf liner he had found. "They looked quite nice." One drawer held nothing but diapers. "Now, can we find something to eat? I'm starving."

She grinned, "I heard your stomach rumbling. For a minute I thought someone was on the drive."

"Funny.' He was raiding the refrigerator. "I have lunch meat, cheese, chips and dips. It's not a fancy restaurant but, oh yeah, bread. Condiments? Water or tea?"

"Water." She watched as he played host, selecting paper plates, napkins and two bottles of water.

"What's next?"

She eyed the clock on the wall. "Sleep, I think. Nurse said sleep when the infant sleeps."

He was stymied for a minute. "You take my bed. It has fresh sheets. I'll take the couch." They finished eating and as they were putting things away, he ask, "would you like something more comfortable to sleep in? There's just a few of Mother's clothing items in her room, if you'd like to see if there's anything...I mean, if you want to. They won't fit but you might be more comfortable."

She glanced down at the slacks she'd chosen that morning and one of her nicer blouses. "That's nice of you to think of me. I'll take you up on the offer. Where is your mother's room?" He pointed to the hall. "Opposite direction of mine. You could sleep in there but I think, anyway, my thoughts are we can hear Abby better from my room than down the hall. She has a small veranda the reason she was down the hall. There's a bathroom to either room if you want to shower, there are a few of her things left in the cabinet under the sink."

"You go first," she said, that way you will be here..."

"You," he said, wagging a finger, "are afraid I will go to sleep if you go first and you don't want to have to waken me." Later, finished with a shower and wearing comfortable clothes, she found him asleep on the couch. She had to smile; they were wearing matching gray jogging suits.

❦

What was that sound. She awakened to the dark but saw the light beyond the hall. Where was she and what was it? Knowledge hit about as fast as she swung up and off the bed, running to hover over the bassinette. Gathering Abby to her shoulder she felt the lump of diaper beneath the gown. The mewing sounds stopped when she picked her up.

With Abby on her left shoulder, she turned the tap and waited for the water to get hot, letting it fill the large cup before sitting the bottle in. The formula was ready by the time she changed Abby's diaper. From where she sit in the arm chair, she saw Jake patting the pillow and she giggled. No doubt he was having a dream and she wondered if it was about the new baby. When Abby lost the nipple due to her wandering attention focused on Jake, she gave a mewing hungry cry.

Jake shot up, his legs swinging off the couch, feet on the floor, a completely confused look on his face before he gained his bearings and saw her sitting, feeding Abby. Energized now that everything appeared to be all right, he came into the kitchen. "I think I was dreaming of her, but I just couldn't get it together when I didn't hear the sound any more. She was crying, wasn't she?"

"Maybe. It's a funny little mewing sound, like a lost kitten. I'm surprised I heard."

"It worries me that I won't."

Amanda chuckled. "I have a feeling that mewing will turn into a full-sized lung exercise. She will blast you out of the bed. So don't worry about it, babies have a good set of lungs."

He glanced at the clock. "I may have to marry your mother. Do you think your dad would notice?"

She had left her phone at the office and now she wondered how she was going to get home and to work on time. He had to meet with the funeral director. That would be a problem too. Who would keep the baby? He wasn't ready to go places with a child. She wished she had a free day to help with Abby, but she didn't. She waited until he was asleep. Her mother was an early riser. She would borrow his phone and call Phyllis. Afraid she wouldn't wake in time she made the bed and dressed. At least she was clean. She could tell Jake's mother had nice taste but most of her belongings had been taken from the room. The one thing she thought would come in handy was an old-fashioned wood rocking chair. The oak had a nice worn look and she wondered if Mrs. Turner rocked Jake in that chair.

At five o'clock she quietly lift his phone from the coffee table in front of the sofa. She text her mother. *Mom, I left my phone at the office. Could you pick me up and if you don't have plans today, Jake has to meet with the funeral director and I don't think he's ready to carry Abby around, do you? He's a bit frustrated. Take the second drive to the back entrance. Thanks, Mom, I love you.* Gently she replaced the phone back on the coffee table but not before seeing he had a number of calls from someone named Belinda.

There wasn't any doubt her mother would be there soon. Amanda searched her purse for a small zippered make up bag she always carried and quickly applied a light foundation, eye shadow and mascara. She ran the brush over the tips of her lashes and dropped the case back into her purse.

As she had known, her mother pulled in to the drive at five minutes to six. Amanda closed the back door quietly and climbed in the car with her mother. "Hi, do you know what it means to have a mother you can count on? Terry and Amy Lou never had that. Thanks, Mom." She leaned across and stretched to kiss her mother's cheek.

"What in the world are you wearing?"

"My guess it was Mrs. Turner's jogging suit, anyway it was in her room. Funny thing is when I came out in it, he was wearing a replica." She laughed. "I think I'm a bit spacey, you don't sleep much with a new born, do you?"

"What's this about Jake having to meet the with Sam Watson?"

"Who is Sam Watson?"

"The owner of Watson Funeral Home and Crematory."

"Oh, he has to make the final arrangements for Terry and Amy Lou. Will the people expect a full-fledged service, with visitation and all?"

"If Terry and Amy Lou left a will and adoption papers with an attorney, it stands to reason they also left instructions in the event they needed a funeral service."

"I hadn't thought of that. Do you plan to help with Abby today? You could tell him, Mom, and remember to call the baby Abby." Phyllis gave her daughter a strange look. "Funerals cost a lot, don't they? Did you know Jake sings and plays the piano? I wonder if he will sing at the funeral?

"Jake often plays at church, Amanda. I think it would be a short distance and good training for Jake to bring Abby to me today, don't you? I doubt with this wet ground he can get in the fields. He has a lot of adjustments to make. He hasn't seemed to date since he and Belinda broke up."

"I wondered if he had anyone special. He said he might ask you to marry him because he needs a wife." Phyllis found that statement funny. She gave a deep laugh. "He said you can do anything."

"Did he ask if you had anyone special?"

"No, and I don't."

"You want to run in at your dads to dress and then I'll drop you at the office?"

Chapter
4

....

Jake was ahead of her and Phyllis. An hour after she arrived at the office, she heard a commotion and went to the door to find what it was about. There stood Jake, one hand clutching a diaper bag and the other the infant car seat the hospital loaned for Abby. Surprised, she hurried to his side. The men had the front covered, every one of them acting as though they'd never seen a baby.

"Hey, Jake, I'm open for being god father, you need a sitter, whatever I'm here." Whoever yelled the offer was being second guessed by the others. Amanda ushered him into her office.

"What's up?"

"My phones out. I have a nine o'clock meeting with Sam about the arrangements. Can you keep her for an hour or two? I'm late." She was shaking her head yes as he went out the door, calling over his shoulder, "She had a bottle at five that last til about six. Thank you."

She placed Abby's carrier on the desk and pulled the heavy blanket away and left the small light weight one. Sleeping like a top, she couldn't help but stare. Such perfection, she thought, rosebud lips and long lashes. One day she would melt hearts. Evidently, she already was melting hearts. Now, she didn't want to study the ledgers; she wanted to sit and hold Abby.

Sadness washed through her, that anyone would not want an innocent baby and Amy Lou and Terry had no choice in the matter. She hoped Jake's time with the funeral director went smoothly. On her way past the men to her office she heard the word, go fund me, but that didn't mean one was started. If the parent's had not thought that far ahead, someone would need to help pay for the double funeral. Baby Abby was making those mewing sounds. She glanced toward the coffee maker with a pot of water and a clean cup sitting beside it. That would do for warming the bottle of formula.

Jake called around eleven. "Amanda, there's been a hold up. I'm still waiting. It seems Mr. William's died. He's elderly, around ninety. Don't know if you remember Mary Jane from school, his youngest. Anyway, Sam's tied up with his family. You want me to come get Abby?"

"I didn't know it took that long."

"Not usually but there's a lot of family here on the William's side and they can't agree on anything."

"Then it's a good thing I'm not with you. We might have a problem, too. Take your time and don't worry, Abby is sleeping sound as can be."

"You won't get anything done."

"I already have." She smiled, not telling him she was content to sit and hold Abby.

"If, you are sure."

"I am." As he hung up, her mother called.

"Have you heard from Jake? I haven't been able to reach him. I guess he's taking Abby."

She didn't get a chance to tell her mother she had Abby, before Phyllis hung up.

It was hard to concentrate on work with a baby as large as life sleeping on top of the desk. She found herself waiting for Abby to wake up hungry so she could hold her and if she didn't wake up soon, she was afraid she was going to hold her anyway. So, she thought with a resigned sigh, this is what all women want to do, hold a baby. A tear formed to trickle down her cheek. Who said life was fair? The words had formed before she could stop them and it seemed she had no control over the tears. Hadn't she cried all the way from North Carolina to Memphis. For some odd reason she thought of the motel and Lois and James Ferguson. Mr. Ferguson had followed her to the car. "We don't have family," he said. "If you ever want to come back to see us, we would love having you."

She had hugged him for the kind words, it seemed he needed a hug. Hadn't she been in that spot?

Taking the ledgers, she began to run the list of supplies purchased, the cost and where purchased. It was eight o'clock when Jake brought Abby and now as she heard the soft mewing sound she glanced at the clock on the wall. Ten o'clock. Just as the night, Abby needed feeding this first week of life about as regular as the hands on the clock rolled around; at least every two hours.

Turning on the coffee maker to let the water heat, she then poured it into one of the big cups and sit the bottle inside. When Woodsey opened the door to tell her a package had arrived he saw her sitting holding Abby. "Now, that's a picture," he said. "You look like a natural. How's it going?"

She gave him a dubious smile. "You tell me. Do you feed them a certain number of ounces before burping, or let them breathe in between, or what?"

Woodsey scratched his head. "As I recall, when they're this little you are rather sparing, better to let them breathe and see how they're doing, don't you think?"

"Why not." She raised Abby to her shoulder, rubbing her back. Nothing happened.

"Try gently patting her back," Woodsey offered. She did as he suggest and in about a minute, they heard a burp that sound to Woodsey a lot like a cat gagging. "There you go. You did it. She did it."

Woodsey left the package by the door and went back to work in the shop area. Amanda was enjoying holding Abby and didn't hear the door open again. It wasn't until Jake cleared his throat in an effort to gain her attention, and ask, "Are you holding our baby?" He was pleased. She could tell by his smile and as if sensing his presence, Abby did a little movement.

"Pull the chair around here so we can both see her and tell me about the arrangements."

He was shaking his head. "I was surprised. Amanda, the kids had thought of everything, almost as though they had an idea something could happen to one or both of them." He sighed. "You'll see at the funeral. In case, there was a letter with full instructions and, get this, Amanda, letters

49

to their child for later. I couldn't believe it. Sam said Amy Lou and Terry came in together and apologized but they wanted to make arrangements in the event..." His voice grew husky. "Sam said he had never seen such devotion to an unborn child, or if it should happen to be one of them."

"So, it went easy." She was feeling Abby move each time Jake spoke. She glanced at Jake. "Watch what she does when you speak." She grinned. "I do believe she has grown as accustomed to your voice as she probably did with her mother's when she was in Amy Lou's stomach. "You want to hold her?"

"Sure, why not?" Jake took Abby into his arms and accepted Amanda's chair.

"I don't believe I've seen a baby riding shotgun on a tractor, yet, but this may be the beginning of something new, for you, anyway." He gave her that look that she was beginning to understand meant there's one more thing I need help with. Tilting her head, she looked straight into his eyes. "What now? I feel you are hesitant to voice something."

"Either I have to ask you to keep Abby, do something necessary, or number three, go with me."

"If we can go after work, I'll take choice number three. What is it?"

"Go to the house for things Abby will need." He dug into his shirt pocket and pulled out a folded paper. "Here's a copy of the list Amy Lou gave Sam to include with other papers for the attorney."

She scanned the page. "It seems pretty much complete except I don't see clothes for their burial on it."

"Not needed, they are to be cremated and the service will be a memorial this coming Sunday."

Amanda sit in the folding chair. "It kind of gets you, doesn't it, that they were so thorough?"

"Yeah, I agree." He passed his free hand over his eyes, "I have become a teary eyed ..." he searched for the correct word. "I started to say fool, but that will never apply to this baby. Look at that." Abby was asleep again and for all it appeared, she had her hand wrapped around his thumb. "I mean, what would you call it? Terry came with a lot of problems, but he was serious about overcoming the bad habits and when he fell in love with Amy Lou, well...he was more determined than ever to be a better man...

the only fault was he liked to drive fast and you can't do that..." His words ebbed down to a whisper. "I guess he proved that, didn't he?"

"You were good friends, that was enough to make you sad, then they both trust you to raise their child." She leaned in to look closer at Abby. "Did you and Terry bear any resemblance? Because this baby might have a few that will make people think you are her biological father..."

He groaned. "Much as that would please me, it could mess with my reputation."

"What? The age you are and you are a lily-white cowboy, no mistakes in your life, speeding tickets, etcetera?" She laughed. "I find that hard to believe."

"You can believe it. I'm a deacon in the church, which means I've got to stay pure." He struggled to keep composure as she stood with her hands on her hips eyeing him as though she didn't believe him. "Okay, so once, I had a wild streak but there's no little Jake or Jukenia's running around. How about you?"

"That's a really tender subject, I'm surprised I would tell you, but I was engaged to a man that told me at last minute there would be no children in his household, he didn't have time for them. We were practically at the altar."

"Not the best timing, huh?" He was studying her, sensing there was more. "Is he likely to show up here? I mean, is there still a tie between the two of you?"

"No, we had our sad farewell, sad for me that I didn't realize how self-centered he was from the beginning." She tried to brush how serious she sounded aside. "I made a mistake. I thought he was the perfect choice and maybe I could forgive that he didn't realize I had a say in whether we had children or not, but that was just it, he didn't see that I should help make the decisions. As much as it hurts me to say, it was nearly the hour we were to be married he told me and I had to make a quick decision."

"How hard was it to continue working with him after you called off the wedding?" He was watching her pace back and forth as she talked.

"It wasn't because I left and came here, you might want to say beat down...I don't know...I stopped to spend the night in Memphis and ran on to this motel owner whose wife was terminally ill and I saw his devotion, trying to work and trying to care for her and it made me think, my guy would never take care of me. It was all about him… As tired as the owner of the motel was, he was still taking care of his wife's needs. A woman needs to see that in the man she is going to marry."

"You told him you were leaving?"

"No. I just left." She stopped pacing and faced him. "Do you think I owed it to him to tell him?" She began the pacing, again. "I don't. But, since we are in confession mode, tell me what happened that you aren't married or at least have someone on the line."

He shrugged, "I guess I haven't found the right one, until your mother and she's taken."

Amanda was close enough she swatted him. "That's pitiful. You won't bare your soul and you of all people know my parents don't live together. They seem to love each other, but they're happy as is."

"So," he asked, "Is that a case of can't live with them but can't live without either?"

She shook her head. "I give up. You aren't telling me anything about yourself…"

"The most important thing is this, I ask you to marry me and I'm interested in your mother."

She rolled her eyes. "Much as I love your little baby, if I'm going with you later, you must go home and let me do a little bit of work and then I'll be ready if you want to drive by and pick me up."

"I got a call from your mother…"

"I'm not surprised."

"She is going to come to the house, rather than my having to take Abby out early."

"That doesn't surprise me either."

"I believe you are going to fit in here, just fine." He grinned. "You might even decide to marry me."

"You really think you need a wife to be mother to Abby, my friend, but I'm here to tell you, if there's no love, it won't work and you don't know me, therefore you cannot love me."

He gave her the look of a man on the prowl. "I tell you what, give it a chance. I think you and I could make a good marriage. I like you. You have already proven to me what you are made of but have I proven to you what I'm made of? I want you to think on that. If you can give me a reply when I pick you up, well, that's the best deal so far today."

"Have you heard if there's not love we are as sounding brass and we gain nothing?"

"Yeah, I have," he said. "I also heard, love is patient, love is kind, it is not self-seeking and the heart of it all is if I do not have love, I have nothing. First Corinthians chapter thirteen. Right?" He rose to prepare for taking Abby home, but stopped to give her a searching look, "Remember what your momma and daddy said? You could do worse."

"Listen, Cowboy, this girl is going to hold out for love. Two people together without love might kill each other."

"I tell you what I'm going to hold out for, I'm going to see where this is going."

She placed the strap of the diaper bag over his shoulder and that's when he bent his head and kissed her. Startled, she left her hand on his shoulder and stared at him. "You keep doing that."

He threw his head back and gave a joyous laugh. "There must be a reason."

When they were out the door, she shook her head as if to clear the reason, as he said why he kept kissing her. Trying to get her mind off Jake Turner she opened the package to find some very unusual items that she had no idea whatsoever what they were. She walked out to the area where the men were working on a particular piece of equipment. Woodsey came to meet her.

"How was your evening of baby-sitting?"

Amanda couldn't keep from smiling. "She's a good baby. I'm trying not to fall for her."

Woodsey grinned. "I have a feeling it's too late for that. What's in the sack?"

"You tell me." She gave him the sack and watched as he smiled and began counting.

"Just when we need them. They're for the sprayer. We were very doubtful we'd get them. Thank you."

"All's well, then?" He nodded and turned back toward the other men.

She returned to the office, thinking she'd finish the ledger, but she couldn't concentrate. It was not in her plans to become involved with another man. The sting Clark left on her should last a while.

Finally, she picked up on the listings she was making in a new ledger, and then she heard a knocking sound. When she checked, the men had all left and Jake was standing outside trying to get in. She heard him calling but instead of going to the door she went to the window.

"Do you mind coming out. That way I won't take Abby from the truck until we get there."

"Okay, I'll be right out." She closed and locked the window before joining him.

"Thanks, I'm trying to get the hang of this parenting thing. What do you think, so far?"

"Good. You have her covered in the heavy blanket. I assume her parents' home has heat."

He gave her the look. "Of course, I wouldn't take our baby into a place that wasn't heated."

"It's amazing all of you lived so close to each other. That's farming territory's way, isn't it?"

They were at their destination in a matter of minutes. Jake slid out of the truck, reached for Abby's carrier and led the way to the front porch of Terry and Amy Lou's home. "Come on in. Amy Lou was always a fantastic housekeeper. I doubt a thing will be out of place."

Once inside, Amanda looked around. "They have managed very well," she said. "It's expensive putting a first home together. I'm impressed."

"Let's start with their bedroom." Again, Jake led the way. "Here's the list and Amy Lou's description of all things. I think that middle door in front of you will be Abby's closet." They worked for an hour, with Abby asleep when he called to her, "Doesn't she need a pretty little dress, for tomorrow?"

"I'm sure they have done her proud." She picked up a framed wedding photo of the two.

"Come see what I found. I guess Amy Lou got it for a special occasion. But it's not pink."

They stood admiring the dress, Jake had laid out on the bed. It was a medium blue with white lace and two tiny pink rosebuds on top of white ribbons on each side of the yoke that dropped down into fullness. "It's so tiny," he whispered. "I can't believe anyone makes clothes this little, and look at this. Here's a small box inside the one that held the dress and look here." He held up tiny white shoes. "And these socks, Amanda, look, more lace. I am overwhelmed. Where were they going?"

Their eyes met and it seemed only natural when he took her into his arms and she lay her head against his shoulder. After a minute he kissed the top of her hair and they went back to work. Jake had been carrying the boxes to the truck and this was to be the last. Abby was moving inside the carrier and Amanda was thinking it was time for her evening feeding. "I think we need to hurry, Jake, our baby is making those mewing sounds, let's go so we can feed her at your house."

"Do you think you could hold her the short distance? The back is full to the ceiling." They were pulling into his side drive in fifteen minutes time and Abby was gearing up for an all-out wailing. "Man, I haven't heard that," he said. "I won't know what to do if I'm by myself with her."

"Probably she will do this one time and after that be her docile little self." But that was not proving to be the case. To top it all off, Abby's crying was making Jake nervous. "Hang on little baby don't you cry; you will hear Daddy singing by and by." Staring down into the baby's little eyes, Abby slowed up but she didn't stop, except to swallow and go again. "Now you have me singing. We must be desperate," Amanda sang in a sing-songy voice, "maybe you are now Abigail showing your other side to us." The crying changed pitch and the two trying to contain the crying looked at each other in desperation. "How does that sound come out of such a little person?" Her singing had turned squeaky.

Shrugging out of her jacket, Amanda hung it on peg inside the kitchen door but she laid her purse on the side table to the sofa. Her phone was in her pocket to call one of her parents later to come for her if everything went well.

Jake sit down to the piano and began to play. Abigail did a little hiccup. Amanda watched as the baby's eyes grew large and she listened. "Hush little baby don't you cry..." Jake was singing and his baby was listening. Amanda began to laugh. "This is the most amazing thing; I've ever been part of. I always said if I had a baby, I would play music for my child while in my stomach so she would appreciate it later and I truly wonder if Amy Lou did." She couldn't resist taking a picture.

Two hours from the time they pulled in the drive, Abby was fed, diapered and finally asleep. "She's exhausted." Amanda said. "And look, she is angelic, those little hands in her prayer mode."

Jake sank onto the sofa. "I'm exhausted, too and I very much doubt I look angelic. Let's see what you look like." She turned to face him. He begin to laugh. She blew a strand of hair away from her lips. "You kind of came unraveled, too." He pointed to the mirror on the wall adjacent to the piano. "Look."

Her make-up had run. She now had dark circles under her eyes and her hair that was in a pony tail of sorts, was loose strands around her face. "I'm a mess." She fell onto the sofa beside him. "But," she raised one arm in the air, her finger pointing toward the mirror, "I earned this disarray."

"Yes, you did. Thanks for staying with me."

"I couldn't leave."

"That's right." He turned to sit where he could better see her. "If you had wheels, would you have?"

"No."

"Why not?"

"I think I'm getting attached to the little squirt."

He was beaming. "Good. I thought you were going to say cry baby." Turning serious, he asked, "What am I going to do if it happens again?"

"Call me, or...play the piano?"

"I am taking a lot of your time." He sighed heavily. "This is something I never dreamed happening and I have no training, at all. No nieces or nephews. With Terry as my best friend, their baby was to be my god child... and we all teased that together we would learn about babies." He sounded so remorseful she looked to see. "Well, it didn't happen, did it, two more days until the memorial."

"I'm truly sorry." She hung one arm over his back, her hand falling just over the shoulder and whether it was because she was tired or a fit of silliness hit, she tickled under his chin, then tweaked his ear. "I couldn't resist that," she said as he pulled a straight face, his eyes were pinpoints. "You were looking and sounding too serious."

"That's how I get my dog's attention," he replied. "So, I don't quite know how to respond." He took a deep breath as he stood and offered her a hand to join him. "You know that little dress, what's that little round thing hanging on the hanger? It's too small for a belt." His chin was nearly resting on his chest. "All I've done the last days is worry. What if I can't get her dressed for the memorial?"

"Do you want me to come help? I will."

"Would you? I hate to impose, again." He grabbed her and danced around the room. "You are so kind to help me like this." He began to sing, "Aman-da, who helps with the kid, don't know what I'd do if you didn't but you did…" How's that for a new lyric? Oh, come on, you started this, didn't you?"

He had that look again and she knew, he wanted to kiss her, but did she want him to?

"That's how I pet my dog." He explained, "The tickling my chin and scratching behind my ear."

"I didn't know you have a dog."

"I do. Her name is Rosemary."

"Rosemary. It's a good thing you didn't name your new baby Rosemary, then, isn't it?"

"I wouldn't." He huffed, acting indignant. "Did we eat? I must be in love to forget that." He danced her around the room and did a grand dip until she was leaning back level with his waist, and that's when he bent…but just as she about closed her eyes he raised up. "Ah, ha. I fooled you, didn't I?"

"You are wicked."

"Hungry, too." Taking on a Dracula voice, he intoned, "Come with me, my lady. It's the frig for you."

"I thought so. It's cold body's for you. Myself, I like warm bodies, can't you tell?"

"Now that you have brought it up, how are you, as you said," she twixt her fingers, "a deacon in the church and it sounds like, by your words, there have been sexual escapades."

"Sounds like," he corrected. "I didn't say I have partaken of the flesh." Putting his thumb and index together, he continued, "but I was this close when thunder and lightning rose all around me and I didn't." He made that face and she pulled out the phone and took another picture.

She was laughing. "I don't know when to believe you or not. You are crazy."

"Let me see, I am, too serious, wicked, weird and crazy. Is there anything else before I am paranoid from being humiliated?" He had suddenly turned serious. "Am I also, a hardworking, likable, reliable, probably lovable and seriously fond of the person standing next to me, kind of guy? Help me out, here." She could tell he had truly become serious. "I take my being ask to serve as a deacon in the church seriously. I guarantee you, at least it is my opinion based on I grew up around here and boys have a way of knowing what other boys, guys, men in the community have linked to their name and the men I serve with serve because it is an honor to be asked but there's not a saint among them."

"I apologize. I should never have called you those names even in jest. I thought we were both teasing along to get through the iffy times with Abby." He was leading her to the kitchen; pulling out a chair and seeing that she was comfortable, as one could be in a straight- backed chair. "Am I forgiven or is this where you find the sharpest knife and silence me?"

He shuddered. "Don't even joke about that. I have that knack. If I get quiet, people don't know what I'm really thinking. I dated a girl once, that let's say we became so, well we thought we were in love but evidently, we weren't because we aren't together, are we?"

"What happened?"

"I don't know. We considered playing house but my mother was alive then and it would have embarrassed her to no end. She was of the old school, nothing sexual until you had a license to say it's legal. But, don't discount whether I'm a true red blooded American boy."

"Since your convictions of what a deacon is, runs so high, maybe I worded that wrong, if you messed up, what would you do?"

"Step down." He was placing a new package of bologna, cheese and bread on the table. "Would you rather have crackers?" She nodded. "Pickles?" He searched the shelves and brought out pickles with a package of chips. "Water or tea?" He found two bottles of water. "Now, dig in to this gourmet delight." He glanced at the clock. "How about you drive my truck home?"

"Let me think about that."

They ate in silence and were finishing when the silence broke. Abby didn't start with the normal mewing that said she was hungry; she gave a wail and kept it going. "I think we are about to have a repeat, what do you think?" Jake was already hurry to Abby's bassinette. "What is it, wet diaper, hungry. Is that a hungry wail?" Amanda was checking the diaper and nodding. He gave her a diaper. Even diapered and dry, Abby didn't stop crying. Amanda took her up, holding her close to her body, her hand on Abby's back, crooning words of comfort, except Abby wasn't comforted.

"Just as well warm another bottle and we probably should count how many are left, at least to know the number she takes in a day's time. I didn't know a hospital had those little two- or four-ounce prepared bottles. That is amazing and so wonderful for new parents, don't you think?"

"Is that what we are new parents?" Jake's glum voice told just how tired he was. He watched Amanda take the rocker.

"Stretch out on the sofa and if I need you, I'll let you know." He started to protest. "I'm good," she said. "If I see I need to stay, I'll call dad." He did as suggest and before Abby finished the bottle, he was asleep. Amanda made the call. "Dad, I'm helping with the baby. We don't know why she's crying."

"Don't sound so worried, Hon," Dad said. "If you're worrying what I think, it's not important. I trust you and Jake, and if you need me to come for you, just let me know. I can do it."

"You know me, don't you, Dad. It's a little soon to worry about us, but thanks for your trust. You're great, Dad." She felt a little more at ease and smiled that he put her concern into words. "I love you."

She rocked an extra hour after the bottle was finished before Abby went to sleep but when she tried to lay her down, Abby seemed to know the minute she approached the bassinette. Finally, Amanda went into the bedroom, managed to pull the coverlet to the end of the bed with one hand while holding Abby in her arms, wide eyed, those eyes locked on Amanda. She had seen a cotton housecoat hanging on a hook behind the door and with care slipped out of the slacks and blouse and into the housecoat. She was growing so tired she was afraid she would drop the baby. From the bathroom she found two large bath towels and stretched them full length, one on top the other and rolled them long ways until he had a divider, she placed between her and Abby that she would feel if she should roll in her sleep.

It was for certain Abby wouldn't roll. With Abby wrapped in the light blanket, she pulled the sheet up and keeping her hand on Abby, talked to her until Abby's eyes closed and she took a deep breath, thinking she would take a shower and then decide what to do about the sleeping baby.

Jake didn't know why he was awake just past midnight. For a minute he wondered why he was on the sofa and immediately he remembered Abby. Jumping up, he was within feet of the bassinette. The baby. He had lost the baby and he couldn't remember where he left her. He began to retrace the places he had visited that day and that's when he heard the little sounds, not the mewling of a new kitten, it was almost a smack or a…he got it, it was Abby, but where was she? He followed the sound and found Abby, eyes open, moving her head as if searching. Searching for the bottle. His elation was so profound he could have jumped up and down, she wasn't lost; he had found her.

Sound asleep, her hand on Abby's body, Amanda's clothes were on the end of the bed and she was wearing the old housecoat of his mother's he had washed and hung back behind the door where she kept it. He smiled. Amanda Lanis was some kind of woman! She would make someone a good wife. His smile widened. She wasn't ready for the deep commitment, evidently, as she sidestepped all such talk. Gently he removed her hand from Abby's body, Abby protest but when he put her on his shoulder and went to the kitchen the bright light subdued her enough time for the bottle to warm.

He sit in the rocker and waited until she emptied the bottle, burped and was ready to go back into the bassinette but that's where the good little baby declared ill will. Every time, as before, when he tried to lay her down, she began to cry, ready to break into a wail. Finally, not knowing what to do, he returned Abby to the bedroom, laying her opposite Amanda with the rolled towel in between but she was awake. What to do? He didn't want to awaken Amanda. He took a page from Amanda's book.

In his bathroom was two bath sheets. He rolled them as Amanda's towels were rolled, to place them between Abby and himself, thinking surely, he would not cross the line. Abby was watching him. He put a finger to his lips and mentally without a sound explained, you do your part and I'll do mine. He thought she understood perfectly, she closed her eyes at that moment. Are you asleep? She opened those magic eyes and gave him a stern look. He dimmed the lamp to a glow and lay down beside his new daughter. Is this good? She studied his face and he would not know but when his eyes closed in sleep, she felt it safe enough to do the same. With a sigh, since the pacifier was not available, Abby put two fingers in her mouth and sucked away before she went to sleep feeling very secure and loved.

··

Amanda awoke to the smell of bacon. Abby was still sound asleep. She could only wonder how many times he had fed and diapered the little baby. She hadn't meant to fall asleep, but she was tired and without thinking launched into the deep. Gingerly careful, she swung her legs off the bed and headed for the kitchen. The table was set, orange juice in a pitcher waiting to fill the short glasses and coffee cups were turned up and ready for that wonderful brown brew that was mingling with the bacon.

"Good morning, Sunshine." He bowed, finished emptying scrambled eggs onto the plate of bacon and came toward the table. "If you are ready the foods on the table. Do you need anything? Coffee?"

She nodded. "Coffee sounds great. Hey, I'm sorry I fell asleep."

"No big deal, I did the same." He pulled out a chair for her. "Let's eat before little miss cry baby becomes captain of our day." Sitting at the head of the table and near the stove, he said, "There's biscuits. I have to tell you, we've only had Abby these few days, and I'm eating the legs off the table."

She laughed. "Me too." She took a bite of the eggs. "Mmmm. You are a good cook, but I've got to tell you, I saw those scales, in your mother's bathroom, and I weighed, even with you feeding me every time I'm here, I have still lost a couple pounds. I was shocked."

"It's probably because I've kept you busy. And you moved in to your dad's, that counts." He paused with his fork mid-air, "I was by your grandmother's house and I see someone is working on it."

"Really? I didn't know. Hold that pose. Yeah, that one. Another picture. I'll go by later today."

"Well," he said, studying her a bit longer, "I guess I did away with giving you the day off. Here we sit like some old married couple, when I was trying to let you have Saturday to sleep in and rest up for the memorial tomorrow." His attention was drawn to a car on the highway driving by slowly. "Oh, no, heaven forbid, that looks like our chairman of the deacon's car." He shoved his near empty plate back and was doing a quick job of removing the dishes from the table. "He's known to gossip and I can't let him get a tale out on us. No doubt he is bringing the new pastor out to get acquainted."

"I thought deacons were the type, slow to anger, slower to gossip and all that good stuff."

He gave her a you-know-better-than-that-look. "He's the chairman, Amanda, and he's old."

She was taking her time cleaning up her plate more than she normally would. "My parents are old, does that mean they are likely to…"

"Amanda." He cut her off as he pulled the plate from between her hands. "Please, go get your clothes on or I'll have to marry you on the spot." He was pointing to the bedroom as the car pulled in the drive. "Could you roll the bassinette in with you? I just know she will start crying."

"If we are going to play this espionage thing, then you better hand over a new bottle of formula."

She found the whole thing comical. "You do take seriously being called as a deacon." She two stepped over to him, stood on her tip toes and kissed him full on the mouth. He was in shock. And then just as glibly she put both hands on the low end of the bassinette, rolled it into his mother's room and shut the door as the front door bell rang. But there was a hasty knock, more of a rap, rap rap on the bedroom door and when she opened it a crack, Jake hand in a bottle of formula and in the next minute she heard Jake speaking to someone at the door.

"Why Brother Baumgarten, what brings you out my way? Come in."

She listened long enough to hear Jake being introduced to the new pastor and then her attention was drawn to Abby voraciously sucking on two fingers. Taking her up on to her shoulder, she whispered, "Don't you cry. Daddy might faint and the good Deacon Baumgarten might have to pick him up, or, better still give him mouth to mouth." Thinking of Jake's expression when she kissed him, she began to giggle before she remembered who was on the other side of the door. With Abby in her arms and the bottle of formula in one hand she made a mad dash for the bathroom. "Thou shalt not giggle," she murmured and almost lost it again. "Boy, I must still be sleep deprived," she whispered to Abby.

Abby took all the formula and burped. Amanda had gained control of the giggling but for how long?

Amanda did a mental assessment of where they were, in Mrs. Turner's bathroom, hiding out. She had to smile; she didn't dare launch into giggling again. So, here they were, she needed to return to her dad's, press her meager clothes assortment for the memorial tomorrow and be prepared to help with Abby. Right now, Abby needed a bath and the items she needed were in the bottom drawer of the little cabinet near where the two men were in private conversation with Jake. First things first, she found her cell on the bedside table and called her dad. He didn't answer. She left a message. Dad come pick me up at Jakes but be sure not to drive in if the deacon's car is still here. Don't come before an hour after you get my message. It would be traumatic if he came for her while the pastor and deacon were with Jake. Normal people jumped to conclusions and they must avoid that coincidence.

Mrs. Turner's bathroom had a wall of cabinet, one sink in the middle and mirror above the whole cabinet. She laid a towel on the countertop and placed Abby on the towel, while the sink filled with warm water. "We can do this," she whispered to Abby. "My first to bathe a baby and your first with me." Every time she whispered; Abby's eyes would widen. "You're listening, aren't you? That's good."

"You are such a good girl. You like your bath, don't you?" Amanda whispered as she washed Abby and it was clear, Abby felt better, tiny little mite that she was. "Tomorrow, you dress up in your pretty little blue dress and lacey socks and little white dancing shoes. Yes, you can dance on our shoulder."

The chest of drawers with Abby's clothes was off-limits presently but the diaper bag was on the shelf beneath the bassinette and there was supposed to be a clean gown. Amanda dug deep beyond the diapers and the bib, to find the gown and slip it over Abby's head. "There you go, you are adorable, Yay," she whispered, "I vote for the sweetest little girl, Abby, Abilgail Turner. Jake's daughter." Amanda bowed. "And that, ladies and gentlemen is the presentation of winner #1, Abigail Turner."

Clap. Clap. Clap. "Bravo." Jake's face was wreathed in smile. "Thank you. It feels out of place for a big ole hunk of God's creation, like me, to give the little one a bath. Thank you so much and for tomorrow, too. It's a big thing. There's a lot more going on than we realize, someone questions the giver and the receiver, meaning Terry signing Abby over to me."

"Is that the reason for the visit, on a Saturday?"

"No other reason I could tell. Of course, they handled it very gently and the new pastor seemed at a loss as to anyone trying to think otherwise with a new baby in the house."

"I guess your servant Ness is intact," then, not meaning to sound facetious, "but look at our baby. She loves her bath and I don't blame her. She better be enjoying these times when someone caters to her every whim." She took a deep breath, patting the sheet around Abby. "How about you, Cowboy? Do you ever long for someone to tuck you in, see that your fed?" She grinned, "And all that jazz?"

"For a minute there I thought you were going to say, change your diaper, and I'll have to tell you when I changed that poopy diaper on our little miss, I gagged and went in and lost my breakfast.'

"It always happens either when you are eating or finished eating, doesn't it?" She smiled down on Abby. "I actually believe she is going back to sleep. Wonders never cease."

"Come with me," he motioned and she followed down the hall to his room. "I want your opinion on what I'm to wear tomorrow? He held up a dark suit, in one hand, and sport coat and lightweight trousers in the other. "Honest opinion, no hanky-panky just to get even with me."

"I never would do that, Jake." She studied the two. "It's still cold, even if Spring is drawing closer, and a dark suit wins no matter what other people are wearing. But if you follow the girls…"

"I'm asking your opinion."

"I would go with the navy." She gave him a dubious look, "Of course I have to say that because I left so quickly that all I remember bringing with me is a navy dress with jacket or a red party dress with rumba ruffles."

He whistled, "I vote for the red party dress. No, let's save that for later, maybe Christmas, because if you remember, fall in the country once harvest starts, there's no stopping until Christmas." He saw her countenance fall, a sort of wistful expression she hid quickly. "Why, did your expression change? Was it the mention of Christmas? I saw…"

"It's not a pity party with so much sadness on other people's shoulders, for me…" she studied the floor a minute before meeting his eyes. "I have longed for a meaningful Christmas since my parents divorced…I mean, as a child it was good until Dad brought home the other woman and my mother was lonely and I said, then find someone. Dad did and you are lonely. Do you know what she said?" He shook his head. "For your Dad, Amanda."

"So how do you feel, personally, concerning your life?" His eyes were as solemn as hers.

"I seem to be searching for all the right ingredients to have a home and I won't settle for second best."

He saw she had that teary eyed look and searched for something to make her laugh. "So, you are thinking if I can find a pair of checked pants, I'll be all dressed for…"

She spewed out laughter. "Well, that was unexpected, Halloween, right? Now that tomorrow is settled," She leaned against the bed post, "What about Thanksgiving?"

He grinned, "That, too, but isn't Thanksgiving all gold and orange and…" He listened for a moment. "Is that our little princess stirring?" Together they tiptoed down the hall and into his mother's room. Abby was sucking on the two fingers but she was asleep. He shook his head, mouthing, "Is she hungry?"

Amanda motioned to the hall. "She shouldn't be. By the way, I didn't see a shirt with your ensemble."

"Ensemble? Oh, the suit? How about a small windowpane blue check on white, not too…"

"Preachy, or even deaconish? I agree, completely." He seemed pleased she agreed. "Shoes shined, Cowboy?"

"Yes, Ma'am." She started to pat his arm when he took her hand in his, looked into her eyes and said, "Amanda, thank you. Just having you with me has settled me down. Becoming responsible for Abby; Her parents gone...I can't tell you, for a while I felt unsettled, like...I can't do this...but you make me think I can.

"Of course, you can," she replied. "I imagine you have a whole community at your beck and call."

"That's not me. I can't handle a whole community, too many people in and out, would Abby ever sleep? If it would be hard for me to adjust, then what about a baby?"

"She might have something like the colic, huh?"

"Oh? What's that and what are the symptoms?"

"I hear its like a bad tummy ache and keeps the daddy up all night."

"Is that when the daddy calls the fairy god mother?"

She laughed. "The fairy god mother has to go home. No, don't worry, Dad will be here any minute. So, I guess you plan on staying in today?"

On the short drive back with her dad, he asked, "So how is little Abby?"

"Sleeping right now, but during my call to you last night, she was in midst her very own lung exercise. I never knew a baby could cry so loud or so long."

"Did you get any rest?" He glanced her way. "I noticed you have dark circles under your eyes."

"That could be mascara. I remember thinking I'd feel better if I took a shower but that little girl was short on the trigger, the wrong move and she was crying. Honestly, Dad, I don't remember if I showered or not and this morning, she needed a bath. She smells sweet and I smell soured."

"Don't let this sour you on marriage." She got quiet. "What's going on, Hon? You haven't told me anything but I know you didn't just come home; you had a reason for coming home and I'm glad you did."

"It's a long story."

Charles bristled. "Did he mistreat you?"

"Sadly, we mistreated each other and I just left. I can't live with that kind of atmosphere, Dad."

"You don't have to." Charles hands gripped the hand control that allowed him to drive. "That kind of stuff just takes the ire out of me. If a man can't be a gentleman, he's not worth hanging." He gave a shake to his body. "I can't handle the mess, if I was still young, I'd go down there and beat the heck out of him."

"Clark's a big man, Dad. If you want to straighten out someone, pick on Jake."

"What's he done?" Charles gave an affectionate chuckle. "I'll whup his butt."

"He wants to treat me like his kid sister, keeps kissing my fore head, top of my hair, that kind of stuff."

"Well, Hon, knowing you, if he tried to kiss you like an American boy, you'd probably deck him." They were turning in the drive to home. "What was that about not coming in when the deacon was there? Why would he care? He's okay, you know his land borders ours and Jakes."

"It was Jake, Dad. He said if the deacon knew I was there he might think something was going on between us and he'd have to marry me on the spot to appease a god-fearing man. I think he wanted to preserve my reputation but I'm glad you told me he has neighboring land. Does Dante know?"

Charles nodded, "Yes, Dante knows the operation. He doesn't make waves. Lord, have mercy, about deacon, wouldn't expect that outta' Jake. But then getting a baby the way, he did, that may have Jake upset. It's upsetting enough to me and I don't have a thing to do with it."

"Really, it upsets you, too?"

"The whole community, Hon. We all knew about Amy Lou and Terry having their baby but Jake, well, we know him. You see the difference? He walks among us, calls us all by name. We know him. You know they dismissed services this morning in order to fully honor Terry and Amy Lou this evening."

"I didn't know they ever did that, but it makes sense. So, you feel he will do all right?"

"Not a doubt. He will be just fine. It's a sad situation but just wait, you'll see it will turn to joy."

❦

She called Jake. "Hi, how are things going?" Then she heard. "Is that our baby I hear?"

Frustration sound in his voice. "She's in that crying mode, again. Will you be here, soon?"

"I'll have to bring my clothes to change there."

"Whatever it takes. I'm about to pull my hair out, Amanda. I don't know if I can…"

"Sure you can. I'll be there in fifteen minutes."

"Door will be open. Hurry."

"Charles watched her coming down the stairs. Her arms were full. "Emergency?"

"Yeah, Abby's crying. His nerves are shot…doesn't know if he can do this…that stuff."

Charles grunted. "I understand. I felt the same way and I wasn't alone. He'll do all right."

"Are you serious, Dad?'

"I haven't a doubt in my mind. I know Jake pretty well. Watched him grow up. I'm surprised you weren't paying attention to the boy next door."

"I wasn't much in to boys but now I'm wondering where he was?"

"As I recall, Jake came home every evening to be on that farm. He did play ball though. The difference in age probably made the difference."

"Gotta go, Dad. Love you. See you there."

❦

It was beginning to feel almost normal pulling into the drive that led to the back door. She collected her dress, mini bag of cosmetics and her shoes and hurried. She heard Abby the minute she opened the door. Without a hitch she lay her clothes on the dryer and went in to take a very red and fretting baby out of his arms. He handed her a bottle of untouched formula.

"She won't take the milk?" He shook his head, a miserable expression on his face. She examined the bottle and then put it up to Abby's lips. Abby latched on to it, greedily, but no quicker than taking the nipple in her mouth cried in disappointment. "There's nothing coming out."

"I don't know what to do."

Amanda unscrewed the lid. "Did the hospital send this one? There's something wrong with the nipple, it's completely blocked. Could you check another bottle and warm it, if it's okay?"

Within minutes Abby had taken all formula from the second bottle and was sound asleep.

"She's worn out from crying." She glanced at Jake sitting on the sofa, about as lifeless as Abby. "And you are, too." She yawned, "the two of you make me tired and I was feeling very well."

"I have lost my sense. To think if I'd just took the lid off the bottle I would've known."

"I'm going to lay her down and then you and I are going to make coffee and pancakes."

"We are?"

"We will," she grinned. "Lead the way, Chef. Are you singing at the memorial? If you are, we will go light on the number. I'll master the pancakes, if you show me where things are and you do the coffee and plates."

In a few minutes they were laughing over her rendition of Mickie Mouse and his tractor pancakes.

"They taste pretty good," he said, as they were finishing. "No wonder kids ask for special shapes." He was putting away the syrup and butter as she loaded the dishwasher. "How is it, you still the beast of problems? Thank you again."

"Aw, shucks, go practice your speech, or song, whatever needs practicing."

"Wow. We are the blue family. You and Abby look fabulous and you smell good, too."

"You look pretty nifty, yourself, Sir." She checked him out, carefully," but there's something sticking out of the left side of your collar. What is that?" She pulled a piece of white stock. "Have you worn this shirt before?"

"Nope, it's been hanging there since Mom died. I thought it looked okay for today." He turned to the bassinette, "Are my girls ready? And are you sure you're ready to keep up with our baby?"

"Nah, let's leave her here." She punched him on the shoulder. "Silly. That's why I'm here."

She watched him pick up sleeping Abby and put her in the carrier. "Where's the diaper bag?"

"Oh, it's over there. Diapers, change of clothes and a small blanket."

"Formula? How many bottles will be needed?" He wore a blank expression. "I'll decide," she said. "Do you have notes you will need?" He tapped his forehead. "I see, they are in your head. Good for you. I hope you remember everything you want to say." He didn't reply.

They passed by the spot where the accident happened and saw the police were there. When they arrived at the church it was already half filled with people who wanted a glimpse of the new baby. A table with a white cloth held the wedding photo she had found in Amy Lou and Terry's bedroom and a small photo of Abby that the hospital had taken. One spray of white flowers interspersed with tiny pink roses was the only floral offerings. Someone had done the best they could.

Charles and Phyllis were waiting on the third row but Jake leaned in and whispered, "Would you all mind sitting on the front row with Amanda, because you are going to be acting grandparents."

"We are?" A smile wreathed Phyllis face and Charles was beaming. "Are you sure?"

"If you will," Jake replied. "Phyllis is going to help me with Abby through the week, so Charles, that means you'll be around, too, doesn't it?"

"That's quite an honor," Charles said, gripping Jake's hand.

"I have a little task to take care of," Jake explained. He went to the room behind the main dividing wall where the pastor and music director normally stood and from the music cabinet brought the old hymnals and began to distribute them to the pews. It was almost time to begin when the pianist slid in to position on the bench and looked at the bulletin with the order of service and began to play.

"It's good to see Jake's in control and can do all the tying together of jobs that goes along with this, like leading singing." Phyllis leaned out to speak with Amanda, "Don't you think?"

"You mean he has been asked to lead, along with speak? No wonder he has been so upset this morning." She glanced to where he had sit the carrier after placing Abby in her arms. "I kind of think he is feeling the responsibility of Abby and on the way in, having seen the police are combing the area where the accident was has been traumatic for him."

"He can handle it," Phyllis replied, "It won't be that much different than Sunday mornings."

"Mother, these were his friends."

Phyllis just smiled. "Charles, look at the crowd. This church is going to be completely full."

"Why do I keep smelling food?" Amanda was at a loss to understand the delicious aroma.

"Didn't Jake tell you; they are having pot luck. Everyone wanted it," Phyllis continued. "This is country, Amanda. The people have come to show their support and caring in the loss of two lives but we don't have posh restaurants to go to after the service, the people are very generous and bring enough food for everyone. You'll see, Jake will stay and show off Abby."

Almost, Amanda felt she was being disciplined like a child but there were far too many other things at play to be angry with her mother. She glanced quickly to her father and knew his thoughts were as hers. He winked and she felt better immediately. It wasn't as though she would receive punishment and that amused her as she checked to see if Abby was awake.

"Mother," she whispered. "Please, reach down and get a bottle ready, just in case. The warm one."

The lady at the piano began to play and Jake took a seat by the Pastor and Deacon. When she glanced around it was as Phyllis said, a full house. It was a solemn event even without the bodies in the coffin. It was almost an eerie feeling that pervaded the room. Only after the Pastor thanked the people for coming and turned the service over to Jake, did it seem the people loosened up. But, she thought, it cannot be a happy event, although Jake had said it was a celebration of Amy Lou and Terry's lives and yet she was holding their baby with not a relative to care. She felt like crying, for Abby, for herself and for Jake whose job was to make people feel better.

The deacon prayed a long-suffering prayer and they all suffered through his self-inflicted sorrow.

For some reason she didn't feel good about him, possibly because of what Jake had said. He just looked like a man that could be condescending and she was an expert on that species. The new pastor didn't have a chance and she wasn't certain she would be returning to the church of her youth, boy next door or parents. Having been away, perhaps she had a jaded view of people and places but if she was paid a salary to be able to pay her own bills and take care of herself, she didn't have to stay. Her chin went up in that defiant stage her mother accused her of as a child and again she was amused.

The pianist was standing, and that caught her attention and released her stubborn observance. Jake slid on to the bench. "All right, folks," he said. "If this is to be a celebration of our friends' lives, let's open the hymnals that have the old songs and we will start with page two forty, How Beautiful Heaven must be." His opening picked up the speed and carried the people through, as they lapse into The Old Rugged Cross, and carried their belief right on to I'll Fly Away. "You are singing like you really believe," he said standing," Alleluia, Alleluia, Alleluia." The people were standing with him as they sang without music and Amanda thought how beautiful, the angels must be singing in Heaven.

"You all just have a seat. I want to talk to you." He glanced to where Amanda and her parents were sitting. "Amanda, would you please stand up? Now some of you may remember Amanda. She is a home town girl but she has been working down South these last years until her Daddy, Mr. Charles ask her to come home to run the family farm. But what I want you to do right now, is meet Amy Lou and Terry's little daughter."

Amanda peeled the light blanket away and there was Abby dressed in the little blue dress with the lace and two pink roses on the bodice, sleeping away with all that singing going on, probably sleeping because she heard her daddy playing the piano. Amanda did a cautious study of the people and maybe she recognized a couple. Strangely enough, she thought she saw

Clark and that was ridiculous. He was miles away in New Orleans on the job before the one in Missouri was ready to happen.

"Terry and Amy Lou were the most organized young couple I've known. They had their funeral planned for when it happened, they picked out the songs you all just sang, they made arrangements for their bodies to be cremated and put in those black vases you see on top of that shelf where we put them so they won't be knocked over and last of all," Jake's voice grew husky, 'They chose who they wanted to raise their baby girl if anything happened to them." Tears ran down Jake's cheeks. "I am honored to be chosen. No one says it will be easy. I had no idea, which leaves me to tell you, I will unknowingly make mistakes because I don't know anything about a baby."

"Miss Phyllis, please stand up." Phyllis stood and Amanda sit back down. "This dear lady has agreed to baby sit little Abigail when I'm in the busy time of planting and harvest. Thank you, Miss Phyllis. I truly love you. And Mr. Charles has agreed to be called Grampa, as an active grampa."

"I want to thank you all for honoring the memory of Amy Lou and Terry by being here and before we leave, we will sing one more song together in celebration of their lives. Our pastor read the obituary of both. Our chairman of the deacons prayed a prayer and your thoughts these last days as you have remembered Amy Lou and Terry have enlarged their lives. Now, I have taken the liberty of setting new words to a song I happen to know this dear young couple loved and I would hear Terry singing it as he worked in anticipation of the birth of their daughter. The name of the song, I Loved Her First."

As Jake began the introduction he was saying, "No doubt, Amy Lou said, I loved her first, I held her in my mind a million times while she was part of me. From the moment she started to breathe, I dreamed of telling her fairy tales and tucking her into her bed with ease because she is a part of me." He played the chords beautifully and a pin could have been heard, had anyone dropped it and then he said, "Terry sang in his robust way, I see my girl flying high in the swing, and some ole boy pushing her and making her sing but if she cries, I'll send him away and he can't come back for many a day." But it was the words," A father's love runs deep, he's the boy that loved her first with a place in his heart where there'll be no hurt and he'll see her through the best times and the worst." There was the sound of sniffling and Amanda guessed not a dry eye as they saw the tears on Jake's cheeks.

She changed her mind, maybe for the one who led singing she would consider the church of her child hood, but more importantly, the little girl she held in her arms for she was falling in love with this one. Jake was singing the song as it was written, the chords of the piano rich and powerful. He was such an expert they were singing Amazing Grace in closing as he ask the people to file past the young couple's picture if they wanted to and say good bye.

Amanda and her parents found themselves the recipient of well wishes from many. "I guess people just need someone to bless in times like this," her daddy said. "You've been very gracious to hold another woman's baby through this hardship."

Jake joined them. "Can you spare her a minute or two?" Amanda lay Abby in his arms and he walked over to an elderly couple who stood talking to a pretty black-haired young woman.

"That's Belinda Miles and her parents, Phyllis explained. "She and Jake used to date."

Amanda nodded, "Yes, he told me." She saw her dad roll his eyes Phyllis direction. "What? Am I missing something here?"

"Not that I know," Charles said. "You want to go in and get something to eat? Your mother brought three different things." Phyllis was headed toward the kitchen but she overheard.

"Well," said Phyllis, "you never know, some people don't bring anything, still they stay to eat."

"You know, Dad, I wish I had driven my car, but as usual, I let Jake decide what we drive."

"I'll run you down the road to get it, I need to stop by the house for a medicine I forgot."

"Are you hurting?" She asked as He shook his head. "Oh, you forgot this morning?"

He nodded and put a finger to his lips, "No need in my having to hear the riot act. But let's tell your mother we are leaving and she can tell Jake. Looks like he's busy visiting, anyway."

It was on her way out, a man in a car like Clark's drove past and waved. Amanda shuddered. If there was one thing she couldn't handle right now, it would be Clark showing up, just when she was beginning to adjust to life in the town of her childhood with all the curious people she had known. She was trying to lose the old feelings of defeat; holding Abby always gave her hope for tomorrow.

For some reason she received a call from her mother late evening. "You should have stayed, Amanda, Jake spent the whole time with Belinda. I can tell you have fallen in love with that little girl but if you aren't careful, some other woman will be holding her hand and it may well be Belinda. Jake is hunting a wife. If there's anything between the two of you, you must heed my words."

"Mother," Amanda replied. "I'm taking a deep breath to tell you, there's nothing between Jake and me. He has needed help with Abby and I've complied, that's all. So, as dad has said, "just mind your own business and I'm sure Jake will take care of his. I love you, Mom. Goodnight."

She and her dad had enjoyed a light dinner, but as she cleared the table, she felt he was ready to retire to his room. "The whole thing today was very taxing, wasn't it?" She asked.

"Yes, it has made me weary in knowing I'm facing something like that and I wonder if I have everything in order. That's why it means so much to me, having you home to take care of the business. Everything all right with the men, Dante in particular?' She nodded. "Good," he said.

"Do we need to make time to discuss anything, Dad, one day when you are up to it?"

"Yes, we do and I'm pleased you are willing. So, I'll say goodnight, if you don't mind."

She had changed into pajamas and turned back the bed when the phone rang.

"Amanda, I just wanted to touch base. I missed you. Your Mom said you went with your dad to get his medicine. Are you all right?"

"Sure. I'm fine. You did a great job today. So, how are you and how is our baby?"

"That's just it, I think our baby missed you. Did your mom tell you; she did that crying thing when she woke up? No one knew what to do."

"No, she didn't tell me. I'm so sorry. You were involved and I didn't really want to stay. You know people stare at you and think they know about you but I have actually lost contact with all of them."

"It was awful, finally I left, thinking you might be there but by then you had come for your vehicle." He got quiet then, waiting for her to speak and when she didn't, he ask, "Amanda, I was talking to Belinda…and I wondered if that had anything to do with it, did I slight you in any way, after you being so wonderful to help me prepare for the memorial, because I was so heavy hearted."

"No, I don't remember thinking that, I just didn't feel comfortable staying…" He was waiting. "You ask some really serious questions, Jake, I'll try to be honest here…I guess I needed someone by my side, to stay, and I knew you would be busy, rightfully so, I can't make any kind of demands on you. We have begun a wonderful friendship, completely unexpected and I appreciate it and I don't want to mess it up."

He gave a heart wrenching sigh, "Oh, Amanda, I think I'm falling in love with you, all kidding, aside, and I have this deep gut feeling that someone has hurt you in the past and you are going to be hard to win over."

Self-consciously, she laughed, a terrible warble of sound; he was so honest and forthright, but that was the man she had come to know and appreciate, ten times more the man than Clark ever was, but what if she couldn't last in a relationship, because Clark had hurt her. "I don't know what to say."

She saw Abby every day at her mother's house. Phyllis watched, her own heart aching. "What's going on that you and Jake aren't seeing each other, Amanda? Did you have a disagreement?"

Holding Abby and delighting in the way she was growing, Amanda replied, "no, Mother, we didn't disagree over anything. He thanked me for helping through the Memorial for Terry and Amy Lou and I said I was glad to."

"Abby needs you."

"I'm here, Mother. You are doing a great job and thank you for letting me come each day."

"Pshh. Wherever I am, that's home for you until I'm gone." She turned the conversation, "By the way, how is your dad?"

"He misses you, but says he knows you can't be two places and you are doing a great thing.'

"He can come here. He was put in as active grampa, why isn't he?"

"Did you tell him he can come over? Did you invite him?" Amanda smiled. "I thought not."

Phyllis changed the subject. "You know Jake has all his acreage planted."

"So do we, Mother."

Chapter
6

··

There were occasional times when Jake called. The first time she heard the phone and thought it was a dream, but the ringing continued. She glanced at the clock before answering. Two o'clock in the morning. "Amanda, can you come down? I have a problem; a neighbor called and said one of the irrigation lines has burst or maybe a fox got in it, who knows, the problem is it's running across the highway. It's Friday night and young people are out late; he says its dangerous and also, it's running over one of the neighbor's crop. Can you come?"

"I'll be there in ten minutes." She went in her pajamas, that covered as much as any summer wear. That was the beginning of June. July brought more of the same. It was fox making holes in the plastic irrigation tubing on the gumbo land that he didn't want any more water on than he planned. Abby was awake and thrilled to see Amanda. The only way she managed to get her back to sleep was when she wore down and needed a bottle. Amanda shut the door tight and crawled into Jake's bed with Abby in the crook of her arm, fed, diapered and drowsy but with enough open eye left she wouldn't lay in her own bed. Secure in Amanda's arms, that's how Jake found them and smiled, Abby was curled toward Amanda with two fingers in her mouth content and asleep.

It was almost four o'clock; if he awakened Amanda now, she wouldn't go back to sleep and he suspected she had been awake for most of the time he was gone, he showered, put on a pair of long leg pajamas which he never wore and lay down on his regular pillow with Abby between him and Amanda. Like clock-work he was up for Abby's six o'clock feeding, had her back in her bed, Amanda up and on the road by the time her mother arrived, ready to stay late, today, as he would be running long hours; at least he didn't have to drive down to Phyllis. Morning drop-offs took time.

She had a meeting planned with the men. Dante, invisible man that he was, would give her report on how the crops were coming along. She did wonder about the tractor going out every morning to do bush hogging and general cutting of the grass along the property lines, she was glad he was having it done but she wanted to caution him about Mr. Baumgarten, she always thought of him as chairman of the deacons and her gut feeling that he could be a menace to one's personal society.

"There's a problem stirring," Dante said. Waiting until she said proceed, he studied the yellow pad in front of him. "Mr. Baumgarten was in the shop first thing this morning. I ask him to come see you and he refused." She was studying his serious expression. "Umm, he wouldn't, though I encouraged."

"What did he say?"

"Would you mind if I tell you in private?"

Some sixth sense told her this was not going to be good. "That will be fine. We'll finish here."

"So, what did Mr. Baumgarten say, Dante?" Dante was shuffling around, nervously. "Go ahead."

"He said, now remember this is after I apologized the run off of water where Jake Turner had a pipe break and the water ran across your land, filled the ditch in between and run onto that strip by the road that he wanted to mow today."

"We can't help what other people do that puts us in the middle. That's not that bad. It will be dried out by end of this day. There's more. What is it?" Dante started the shuffling again. "What?"

"He called you names, Ma'am." This is ridiculous, she was thinking. She stared at Dante.

"Names, over water that will dry up by this evening? What kind of names?"

"He said he should've known Mr. Charles was making a mistake putting you in front of the farm."

"That's an opinion. What were the names?"

"It all goes together. I can't say the names to you but he said you're just like your daddy, you don't keep your mind on the farm, you're too busy thinkin' about Jake Turner and probably that baby is Mr. Jake's, anyway."

Confused, Amanda spoke out loud. "Jake and I don't even date but I do help with Abby, occasionally." She studied the wall beyond, "I don't know what he's getting at, but I will talk to him. If you don't mind, don't say anything to the men, why have everyone discussing Mr. Baumgarten?"

"I won't have to, Ma'am. They were all there when he called you and Mr. Jake names."

"All right, Dante. Thank you and keep doing what you are, the crop looks good and tell Woodsey I'd like to see him, please." She was still standing when Woodsey knocked on the door.

"I knew you were going to call me. You want to know what he said. He said you and that Jake Turner are 'horin around and Jake's probably that baby's daddy. I'm sorry, Amanda, you know I am. If he wasn't so old, I'd wipe the floor with him."

"I wonder, what was his demeanor. Was he vicious or calm and said it like he believed it."

Woodsey scratched his head. "He was hot, angry, red face, talkin fast and spit flyin. I'd say he'll be talking out of turn in town, but don't let it bother you. If he'd talk about you, he'll talk about anyone." Woodsey slipped the cap back on his head. "People don't put much store in someone like that. They learn them real quick." He saw tears in her eyes. "Aw, now Mandy, please don't cry."

"The nerve of a man that is supposed to be a leader of the church, but isn't that strange, I didn't like him the first time I met him, I had this gut feeling he wasn't what he pretends to be. I'll pay more attention, from now on, when something in me says something is wrong. I'm glad he thinks we are dating, because if we are it has been months. I think I had one date with him when I first returned."

"Amanda, I need to ask you something. Do you know a fellow that drives a low-slung sports car? I don't know the name but it's black and shiny, like it just got cleaned up, I mean spit polished shining."

"Where did you make that kind of contact?"

"He was by here. The evening after Amy Lou and Terry's memorial. He didn't go through the pumps, he stopped by here and ask where you were and I plumb forgot to tell you."

"It could be someone from last place I worked as I did hear there is a need for some new project in the area. Can you give me something like, what the driver looked like?"

Woodsey thought, "There was this guy, a muscle builder, but he was also big in the world of stocks and bonds according to him. But what do I know about those things? Reckon he was lying?"

For the first time Amanda laughed. "Big in stocks and bonds? If it is who it sounds like, knowing

he messed up, he tried that routine on me." Woodsey was heading out. "Hey, don't you want a first lesson in stocks and bonds?"

"Nope, but I'm glad you came home to your roots."

"Hey, you aren't getting away without telling me how Tina is doing."

Woodsey turned back, his head tilted. "Right now, the experimental drug is working. She hasn't grown another head or anything and we laugh about that; it's just good to laugh."

"Yes, it is. Tell Tina I am rooting for her and I hope to see her soon. Thanks, Woodsey."

She sit down to the desk to gather her thoughts to work with farm matters, it was Clark, no doubt about it. Even in a different automobile, which sounded just like him, low slung and shiny, meant he had spent his hard-earned bonus, every penny if needed on a new sport car and he was somewhere in the area. All she had to do was find out who was building right now.

If nothing else, hearing Clark was somewhere near, reminded her she was to send an address in order to receive the bonus she earned on the last project. As far as seeing Clark, it was inevitable, he would appear the perfect gentleman, waiting for the right moment to demand she perform with him in some god-forsaken high rated restaurant with white table cloths. The singing was her secret. They had started out singing together at the company socials. That would be three years ago, when she and Clark found, quite by accident that their voices were good together, which led to singing locally. She had nothing to do on weekends and Clark found the attention rewarding. Always one to bow to an audience, he immediately decided they must dress the part if they were performing. Amanda often thought Clark regarded himself as much a country ballad singing as Vince Gill or someone popular.

The farm came first and now Baumgarten had to be dealt with. She should tell her mother, before local gossip told her and she was upset with her daughter. When lunch time rolled around, she drove the short distance to Phyllis house to find her dad there. His face lit up watching Abby trying to stand alone in the playpen Jake had set up.

"Look at our baby." Amanda gathered her up from the playpen. "Aren't' you something, standing there like a big girl. I'm so proud of you." Abby was equally proud to see Amanda. She was patting Amanda's face, her smile revealing the tiny white of a new tooth. "Oh, look at you, a tooth shining through. I bet you can bite us, can't you?"

"Don't encourage biting." Phyllis was folding Abby's blanket. "What's new with you?" "I doubt you'll want to hear this. Jake had a problem with a fox making holes in a pipe and the water ran over onto our land and then hit Baumgarten land." She had their attention. "Well, he got the tubing problem fixed but Baumgarten wanted to mow this morning; the ground was too wet but will be fine this afternoon but that wasn't good enough he called both Jake and myself bad names and said probably Abby was Jake's kid, anyway. Will this affect you in church? I didn't think so, but I'm asking. "She saw her mother's indignation right away and her dad's face had turned red.

"The nerve of that guy. I didn't think he was deacon material before our last pastor left and he certainly didn't know. I'll give him a piece of my mind." She practically snorted. "What next?"

Changing the subject, her dad asked, "Are you ready to move in this weekend? If you are take your pick of the men and we'll get it done."

She hugged his neck. "I'll miss you." Then she hugged her mom. "Please don't ever leave me."

"I'll help you if Jake doesn't need me; tomorrow, being the weekend."

Two things happened that afternoon. Clark called. "If you don't talk to me, I'm coming by your office this afternoon."

"What do you want, Clark?"

"I miss you, Babe."

"I doubt that, Clark. You probably want something. What is it?"

"We've been asked to sing at Gains City?"

"No, maybe you have been asked."

"Oh, come on, Amanda, nothing happened that was so bad. You can turn loose of hurt feelings to do this."

"Is that what you call it? Hurt feelings. Your wife shows up, thank goodness, before I marry you."

"I told you, that's over. I have nothing to do with her. She understands that, now."

"What about your son?"

"That is not my kid."

"Clark, the child is your image. He needs you. He looked so lonely."

"No, I won't let her pin that on me. Will you do the gig? It's five hundred for the one night."

"No. I'm going to hang up now."

She had just turned to leave the room when the cell rang again. "I said no," she stopped talking. It was Jake and he was laughing.

"I believe we had this conversation once before. How are you and are you busy tonight?"

"Hi, I'm sorry. A pushy salesman."

"I'd love to cook dinner for you, if you're free."

"I would have to leave early; I'm moving in tomorrow. They finished maintenance on grandmother's house. In fact, I was just going out before they leave to tell the men I need a couple for tomorrow, if I can find two that are willing."

"I'll help if your mother doesn't care to keep Abby, but if that's a problem, I'll ask when I pick up Abby."

"How's it going?"

He sounded a bit wistful when he said. "She misses someone, so do I." When she made no reply he said, "I'll see you later. Is seven all right?"

"Yes, that's good." The third thing, her mother called. "It must be important," she said, "since I just saw you an hour ago."

"It is very important. Are you going to let a good man slip right through your fingers? Because I need to tell you, there are women want him, one I think is Belinda. She is moving back. She lost her job in Los Angeles. You know, she went out there to get in movies. She's pretty enough but word is she can't really take the requirement or nasty talk in the movie she got a part in. She's moving back."

"Yes, you said that. I moved back and it has worked, I hope it works for her, too."

"Amanda." Frustration sound in Phyllis voice. "What do you not understand?"

"Mother would you rather keep Abby tomorrow or help me move in?"

"If that means Jake will be helping you, I'll keep Abby, or maybe if the house is the right temperature, I might could watch her and maybe put things away. Would that work?"

"You would climb a mountain if it meant Jake and I were thrown together, wouldn't you?"

"Probably so." She heard Phyllis laughter as she closed the cell.

She pulled around to the back as the Excavator was still sitting where it had sit for three weeks. He met her at the door. "Hey," his smile was the best thing she had seen all day. "Why the gloomy look," he asked.

"I guess I just as well get it over with. Has Chairman of the deacons, Baumgarten contacted you?"

"No, why would he? Have I done something besides spill water on the road which actually gave his thirsty crop a sip of refreshment?" He wore a puzzled expression, so he didn't know. "You look as if you lost your best friend so I am assuming it is pretty dire, as in awful coming from him."

"It is. Second of all he made a statement in front of our men that Abigail was probably yours."

Jake's eyes seemed to draw into pin points. "I see. And the first thing?"

"He said you and I didn't have our minds on business, not his exact words but the meaning, because we were 'horin." She took one of the kitchen chairs and waited for his reaction.

Jake set a bowl of salad down so hard on the table it jarred a few times. "He came to your men, not me, and talked to them about you...which matters greatly what they think, because what they think of me doesn't matter in this instance, but it matters to me coming out of a fellow member of the church we both attend and I won't have it. He has had a loose mouth for some time now, and I wondered what he had on the last pastor to be made chairman of the deacons. I certainly didn't want to have to deal with church problems, but someone like Baumgarten will run off more people than do good, besides our church reputation won't hold in the community to invite new people in."

"I felt bad about it. Dante first told me but he wouldn't say Baumgarten's accusation of our 'horing.

Of course, it was Woodsey told me and it stressed him pretty bad to tell me. But we go back to my growing up under his tutelage as a teenager." Jake gave her full attention.

"You don't mind if I follow up on this? The man has to be stopped." He reached for the house phone. "We have a few minutes until the roast comes out of the oven." He dialed a number.

Amanda heard Abby whimper and went in to see about her. After changing Abby's diaper she took her into the kitchen. Jake was taking the roast from the oven. "Oh, that looks delicious," she said as he made room for the pan on the table. Then he came over to see Abby. Amanda held her up, knowing he would kiss her. "I bet it's time for a bottle, isn't it?" She watched as he got the bottle of formula and warmed it, handing it to her. "Oh, my goodness, she is excited and ready for it."

"After she's burped, we will put her in the swing. She loves it. Almost five months old and coming right along." He beamed when he talked about her. "Aren't you? My good girl." Abby loved hearing his voice, she kicked her legs and mad cooing sounds. "Let's see if she likes the swing tonight."

He had Abby in the swing in a minute's time and motioned for Amanda to take a seat. "I'm so thankful to have you as our guest, shall we say grace." They bowed and Jake prayed. When finished he said, "Help yourself and see what a bachelor can cook. Like I said I'm so happy you would come down. I want you to know I made a call to our former pastor and he thinks it might be best to go ahead and see an attorney about this latest event and he admitted there will be more incidents like what we are going through as Baumgarten doesn't know how to refrain and it will get him in trouble with the new Pastor but he said it was time for him to move on."

"Are you going to tell the new pastor?"

"I'm trying to decide. If I do speak with him, I think it would be best if it is face to face. He won't want an attorney or the problem to be known outside of the church. The problem with that is Baumgarten is probably talking about what he thinks is true everywhere he goes."

"I'm no help to you, Jake, I don't know either of them. I have to find a church to attend but I don't want to be in with him, if that's how he feels towards us, when he doesn't even know me."

"I would be so happy to see you in our congregation every Sunday and I know Abby would too."

They finished eating and cleared the table. "Have you noticed how good we are together?" His hand was on hers and then she was in his arms and he kissed her.

"You always surprise me; I think maybe a little stunning perhaps to find myself so easily in your grip."

"Oh, come on, grip?" He was laughing. "Was it that bad? I've been wanting to kiss you since you arrived. You have that effect on me."

"What about other women?"

"Nope." She used the dish cloth and snapped it at his behind. "Seriously," he said, side stepping. "Only you." He began to sing, "Only you can claim that power over me," and he was dancing her around the kitchen floor with Abby watching from the swing. This time the kiss was long, lingering.

She came out of it a bit dewy eyed. "I've got to go. Tomorrow will be brutal, moving in."

"What time?"

"Early. Too early for Abby."

"Honey, you have no idea what time this little woman wakes up." He pulled Abby out of the swing and danced around the room with her head on his shoulder, his hand firm upon her back.

"Did she laugh?" Amanda found herself smiling. "Has that happened before?"

He was holding Abby arm's length, amused, "I don't think so. Is five months early for laughing?"

"I don't know. Everything I know about babies started with Abby." She was backing toward the door, "Uh, uh. Don't look at me that way." She grabbed her purse and was out the door, looking back to see he had his nose pressed against the clear glass, mouthing, I love you.

Her fingers trembled as she fumbled with the key. In spite of her own warnings, he was wearing her down. Hadn't she promised herself, it would be a long time before she loved another man?

She was a mile from Jake's when a vehicle pulled onto the road behind her and trailed her the remaining miles to her father's house. Surely Clark was not staying over, his work was fifty miles away. She would not have him spying on her. Without realizing why, her thoughts turned to the talk show she'd listened to when she was driving home from North Carolina and then there was an article she had read about a woman being stalked and the woman's therapist spoke out, saying when a person's mind was messed up, they found stalking put them in a high energy mode. She needed to find that article and read it again, to be certain Clark was not falling in to that category.

Moving day was not the usual, in one sense of the word it was different but in another it was dripping with male hormones. She had not seen Dante' or for that matter, Woodsey in muscle shirts and then there was Jake, who had somehow become the master mind, in agreement with her father. She soon learned, no need giving her own personal opinion. It was her house, her grandmother's stored items, but moving would have a structured quality; theirs. Phyllis added her own brand of finesse to the whole thing. "Have you ever seen such fine bodies? I mean look at those behinds, they could give that male team a run for their money. What's the name?"

"Mother, how would you know about...well, never mind. Just act your age, there's one willing to prove you right. We can't have them or him stripping." She heard Jake's laughter leading the others.

End of day, Charles was practically falling out of the wheel chair. Dante' and Woodsey went home with only Jake finishing the task of applying new paper holder in the bathroom and a safety bar in the shower being replaced due to the holes left by the one her grandmother had used.

"Here we are again," Jake was humming, noting Phyllis had left Abby in Amanda's arms as they were rocking very slowly in the living room, heads together, tired but satisfied. It made him feel all warm and content. His cell buzzed and he answered.

Amanda's eyes were closed but she heard the conversation. "No, Belinda, I'm sorry I can't. I'm tied up, tonight, but yes, I'll see you at church tomorrow." She drifted with the sweet little bundle in her arms but was aware sometime later someone was sitting across from her.

"You are staring. Not nice to watch me sleep. I drool."

"I don't see any drool. You looked quite beautiful."

"Jake." She yawned, trying to come awake. "I bet you are starved. Mother brought a pot of soup."

"I know. I set the table, with your nice bowls and laid out the crackers and cheese. I even made tea." He was beaming collecting Abby. "She will wake up for that bottle, wait and see."

"Where do you get that endless energy? I am zonked."

"You could have moved in with me and spared yourself all this hard work."

"Jake, what would deacon Baumgarten have to say? Living in sin, probably to have a baby out of wedlock."

"I was thinking, first, a solid gold band on the left hand second finger, Ma'am." He grinned.

"Don't you need to go home?"

"I do, but," he crossed the space to her and went down on one knee. "If you need a traditional marriage proposal, I'll do it. Right now." He took Abby out of her arms and put her in the carrier and then he was back, more intense than before. "Amanda, I want to make you my wife, will you marry me?"

Her hands seemed to have a mind of their own, one on each side of her face, a complete emotional stand-off. "I can't." Tears ran down her cheeks. "Why would you want to marry me?"

He pulled her hands away from her face and held them in his own. "I told you, I have fallen in love with you and I won't give up. You don't trust me or you'd tell me why you refuse me on so many occasions. I can tell you've been hurt but in what way?"

"I can't talk about my past, Jake, it's too upsetting. Let's go forward and forget all of this."

"I'm going to give you time, Amanda. You will see me, but I won't bother you in any way. If you still want to love Abby, I can forgive that too."

"You are cutting me out of your life?" She felt the pain settle around her heart the same way it had when her parents divorced. "I know you will be forced to cut me out of Abby's life, too?"

"No, Amanda, we aren't cutting you out of our lives. It's up to you." He saw she was visibly upset as she watched him gather Abby's things. She came to him, her hand out as if to shake hands and he pulled her into his arms. "I know you feel the same emotions, but you won't give in and I can't make you. When or if it happens, it will be with joy in your heart, because you want to." It was a gentle kiss that lingered until the sob broke and she could take no more sadness. She ran to the bathroom and when she returned Jake and Abby were gone.

It was past eight, she was tired but couldn't rest and her work ethics had left with Jake. She stood at the kitchen window staring out into nothing in particular, and hardly noticed when the doorbell rang. It was the pounding on the wooden door got her attention. She glanced down at her worn clothes, as she went to the door. Moving had created a few tears but at the moment they weren't that important.

She had never imagined Clark standing on the porch, waiting to be asked in.

"Why are you here?"

"I needed to see you, to explain."

"There's nothing needs to be said between us, Clark. Just leave. I don't need…"

"Amanda," he interrupted, "let me come in. I promise I won't stay long." He actually stepped around her. Taking a seat, he began, while she stood by the door, ready to turn the lock behind him. "Amanda, I'm sorry. "Please, let's start over."

"Why, Clark, we don't have the same needs, so let's don't torture each other with false hopes."

"About the child, Amanda, he isn't mine.'

"Did you do the DNA testing?" He shook his head. "That's what I thought. He's yours, Clark and it is unforgiveable if you don't acknowledge him as your son."

"Really? Is that all you have against me?" His voice rose a pitch and she edged toward the bedroom door. "I will not acknowledge a kid that is not mine, to be shackled to that bitch mother for the rest of my life."

She thought of Abby and who would be her mother and would that woman feel shackled for the rest of her life, but she said, "No doubt, there's a reason she feels so caustic, Clark, you slept with her and got her pregnant and then declared anything that come out of her wasn't yours. I'd feel the same way."

He clenched his teeth together and she saw the temper rising. "You should leave, now, Clark."

"That would never happen with us. I told you, there will be no children."

"And I said that wasn't wholly your decision. Most women want to have a baby."

"Is that it? really?" He stood, menacing over her. "Or is it that tall guy I see you with. You fell for him. No doubt he's a Southern gentleman and what am I?"

"You're a bully and when you ridiculed me in front of the whole crew and told me I wasn't good enough for you…somehow the *we will have no babies phrase,* was the straw that broke my back. I come from an atmosphere of caring people who help each other, even when they disagree and maybe I'm one of those women that wants a baby. If it kills me, I won't take you back."

He grabbed her, his hands around her throat and would have killed her but neither of them had heard the front door open to know who it was that put a head lock on Clark and dragging him to the open door pushed him out onto the porch and slammed the door between them.

When she saw Jake, she screamed, "he's outside, he might hurt Abby." Jake was out the door as quickly as she screamed. He had left Abby locked in the truck while he came through to have Amanda open the door. Now he free'd her from the seat and pressing her to his chest ran in to hand her over to Amanda, while he made sure Clark left. Jake had seen the marks on Amanda's throat.

Jake jerked him from the open door, slammed a fist into Clark's face and caught him on the rebound pulling his arm so tight behind Clark's back he heard the joints pop. "You touch her again; I will kill u."

"When my lawyer gets through…" Clark gasp, struggling to breathe in order to talk.

"Bring him on," Jake snapped, "otherwise, you, stay out of town."

"Do you know who I am?"

"No, and I don't care. Now, get outta here." That said, Jake walked back to the porch, turned to watch Clark drive away. "Amanda count Abby's bottles with formula." She gave him a puzzled look. "I said count Abby's bottles with formula. It's that simple."

"Don't be so grumpy with me."

"Really? I'm grumpy? That's the best you can say when I walk in on the Asshole trying to choke you to death and you call me grumpy? I swear, I thought your judgement better than that."

"He wasn't always that way." She unzipped the bag and counted the bottles. "Three."

"What did he do different? Slap your cheek." Jake counted on his fingers. "Three plus the dry formula in that little square package will hold her til midmorning tomorrow. We're good."

"Good for what?"

"I'm staying, spending the night. In a few words, I'm sleeping on the sofa. I hope you don't mind because the way I feel right now I thought better of you. Now, that's settled. I am staying."

"Why are you staying?" He had that look that says don't mess with me…but she needed to know.

"Because I saw what was in his eyes. He'll be back and I'm waiting for him." "Oh," She knew Clark would return. He wasn't one for defeat. Already she was trying to devise a plan. "Can I take Abby into my room?" He nodded. Again she made no reply. His attitude scared her.

"So, where's the sheets for this sofa?" He didn't mince words. She found them quickly.

She gave him the sheets and returned to her bedroom. He had not argued about Abby being in her room. They both realized when Clark returned, things could get ugly. She lay down, fully clothed and pulled the bassinette within an arm's reach, that she might comfort Abby, if needed.

The clock was on the dresser directly across from her bed. The hand had settled on midnight when she heard the screeching of tires on pavement; that would be Clark. If, true to old ways he had drank to cool his anger but it would stoke the fire of resentment that someone was there to curtail his treatment of Amanda. Now, he would lay out justice on the one who went against him.

She heard Jake's movement across the room and Clark's heavy foot land on the wooden floor of the porch. She listened to Jake dial in a number on his phone and then he opened the door with such force, Clark fell in to his arms. "You smell like charred wood, where have you been?"

"I'll never tell, but there were several tractors under a shed and a little toy excavator in the yard."

Jake pulled the belt from around Clark's waist and in one movement had it around the man's upper torso with his arms pinned to his side. He then took out his cell and dialed the fire department. She heard him give a location as he shoved Clark out of his way and prepared to leave. "Can you keep Abby? I believe the moron set fire to my home or the shop."

"Not the shop, Big Boy," Clark muttered, "that…" He stopped talking when Jake pushed him out the door onto the porch again. Jerking his own belt from the loops, Jake pushed Clark to the post and brought the belt together behind Clark's back and then Jake left. "Amanda, get me out of these restraints," Clark bellowed, but Amanda closed the door and Clark heard the lock click.

Clark bellowed, and stomped on the porch floor while inside, Abby whimpered. Amanda warmed the formula and sit in her grandmother's rocking chair observing how Abby was growing and how right it felt to hold this little girl in her arms. She was aware when Clark quit calling her name and once Abby was back in the bassinette sound asleep went to the door to peek out. The alcohol must have kicked in, Clark for all the discomfort was laying against the porch post, sound asleep. It was at that moment the Police car pulled in front of the house and the two cops came to get Clark.

"The ending to a busy day," she said aloud, as she lay across the bed waiting for Jake's return. She was asleep when he entered through the back door, found the bathroom in the dark and showered away the grime and ashen smell the fire had left on his skin. He had dumped his clothes into the washer and cleaned the shower when he heard a hungry little Abby sucking her fingers. For a minute he wasn't certain what Amanda might have in the closet he could wear. When he looked, he had to smile, there was his mother's old jogging suit Amanda had worn from his house and he felt maybe he hadn't been forsaken, after all. He pulled them on and went in to see about his daughter.

Whether she had slept too much or was energized seeing him, Abby finished the bottle and would not go back to sleep. He hated to wake Amanda, and finally with a firm grip on Abby, lay her in the middle of the bed, pulled the sheet over Amanda and crawled in on the other side of Abby. Abby's fingers were running over his face, until she put them in his mouth and seemed fascinated with the novelty of his teeth. In minutes she snuggled up to Jake and went to sleep. It was the most comforting night the three had seen in months. Later the adults would be grateful, but not now.

Amanda awoke to find herself snuggled up to a warm pillow, a firm pillow she didn't remember and Abby was asleep next to her, wadded up in the fetal position she seemed to take on when she was most comfortable. Amanda could not remember putting Abby in bed with her, nor did she remember a hairy arm circling her head, a few locks of her hair stretched tight under that hairy arm. Hairy arm? Almost, she wanted to jump from the bed, but in light of the situation maybe she needed to take stock, all things considered. Easing on to her back, she could turn her head and when she did Jake was staring into her eyes, a slight expression of love lighting those eyes.

"Good morning, Beautiful," he said.

"What are we doing?" Shock was the only word to describe her. She had to be reminded it was all okay. "I mean, how did I get in bed with you and her?"

Rising on one elbow, Jake kissed her, long and satisfying. His voice was husky when he said, "It could be this way every morning. I find it quite pleasing. As I knew, you are beautiful."

"I'm a mess. Almost horrified. Tell me," she winced. "When did I take off my clothes?"

"Well, you did remove your trousers but not anything else to be alarmed over." He grinned. "I stopped you. I found that oversized shirt in one of those drawers. It's yours? I hope."

She glanced down, quickly. "Yes, yes. Thank goodness, it's mine."

"Abby is loving it," he said. "We've certainly progressed, haven't we?" He pulled her close. "I guess you wonder what your man set fire?" He tilt his head thinking, "the back side of the house will need a few repairs, actually those things we had decided on, already.'

"But did he burn up any of your equipment?"

"He would have but Dante' came along and seeing I wasn't home he began to try watering down the fire; there's a few pieces that are hard to replace after fire damage but Dante' did good."

"Dante' put out the fire?" Jake was nodding. She was mesmerized by Jake being so close. Jake continued, "He's a good man. He was grimy as all get out. I sent him on down the road. Lord help us all." He brushed a lock of hair away from her eyes. "What happened to your man?"

"He is not my man and like your man, he went on down the road, with two police escorts, of course." She thought of something, "If Chairman of the deacons happened by just now, I'm afraid you and I would be in one of his little sermonettes, where we succumb to his description of life, and roll in the river like pigs, and we would be doomed to hell. I guess I should get on my feet."

Jake gave a long sigh. "You'll have to admit, this is quite cozy, plumb delightful, actually. I love it. Don't you want to marry me and let's play house anytime we want? I'll help with the cooking and cleaning and you can boss me around all day long. How about that proposal?"

Leaning across her body, he checked on Abby and then brought his attention back to Amanda. "Say you will marry me so we can live happy ever after." He kissed her again and she responded. The phone he carried into the house the night before was ringing. "That phone has terrible timing but I have to answer, since it could be the insurance company and now, I have a house to rebuild."

On Sunday it was Jake's turn to open the church doors for the members. After she accompanied Jake and Abby to see the damage to their home. "It seems having the door between the back entry utility room and the kitchen saved your house a lot of smoke damage," the insurance agent was saying. "The utility room is in shambles and the whole outside wall of the house is damaged to the point it is all going to have to be stripped down and let's go outside and talk about the roof." He led the way.

"If that outer wall has to be replaced, there may be a problem with the roof and I can tell you from experience it is hard to match shingles, mainly the normal wear and tear distorts the color. What I am going to tell you is this, be patient and wait for our decision what we can cover." He held up a hand as Jake started to speak, "I know, your parents have replacement value on the policy but right now there are other problems, materials are hard to come by, even when you're due them."

"What about where I stay while the house is undergoing repairs?" He stubbed a toe on the concrete, "I don't know how I'll manage a motel with a baby under a year old."

Amanda clutched Abby tighter in her arms. "I have a room that is empty if you want to move one of your bedroom suits in, I think I could help you with Abby, if you wish."

Jake wasn't expecting her offer. "This may take several months, right Jonathan?" The agent nodded. "Besides that, it might open up talk and I can't have people making assumptions about us." At those words, Amanda hung her head. "Oh, I didn't mean it as harsh as it sounds but this is a little backwards town with little to talk about and they would talk."

"I didn't ask you to sleep with me, Jake. I offered you a room until you need to move on." "I can't have them talking about you. I'm thinking of you."

"Well said," Jonathan busied himself, leafing through the papers in his hand. He was aware something had transpired when Amanda left to return to the truck with the baby. "Did I say something wrong?" He asked.

"No, I did. I just got myself in a heap of trouble. Sometimes it's what we do. Right?" Secretly, his heart ached, he did love her. He had said those words wrong. Would she forgive him? He already realized he had created a bump in their relationship that shouldn't have happened but he couldn't tell her the rest of the story, yet. While at church Baumgarten was waiting for him, to tell him his own version of Amanda helping with Abby, referring to Amanda as some soiled dove, "that woman."

❧

Amanda was at a loss to understand the rebuff she felt she had just experienced. What had happened in those few moments? An hour earlier, Jake was asking her to marry him. Now the picture was clear. He had been playing a game. Her spirit was backed into a corner and as always, she would move on; she learned early in life, to survive others actions you put space and time between them and yourself. She looked down at Abby sleeping peacefully. "I'm going to miss you," she whispered as she wiped a hand across her eyes. "I won't cry but if you ever need me, I'm here."

Later as Jake climbed into the truck, he said, "We are going to have to rush to be on time to church. I hope I have all of Abby's things in that bag."

"I'll dress Abby for you," she said. "I won't be attending this morning."

❧

That afternoon Jake moved to the motel, a dreary little place with its faded comforter and matching drapes. Amanda was glad Abby wasn't of crawling stage. The carpet was horrendous.

"I'll either keep Abby here until you finish moving in or follow and help you. Your choice."

"If you really don't mind helping me move in, I could use your suggestions on how to set up Abby's space." She had followed and seen the austerity compared to his home. It was so depressing she couldn't wait to leave. She kissed Abby goodbye and walked out the door. If there had been any friendship between her and Jake, a stranger would never have known.

Back at her grandmother's house, she saw he had left his work shirt, and in the pocket a small note book with all the employee names that worked his farm. Strangely, she hadn't met any of them. She hung his shirt on the back door nail with the extra set of keys. It was too soon to face him, again, and already her heart ached for Abby.

The following day her mother called. "We missed you in church. Is everything all right?"

"Why wouldn't it be?"

"I don't know, dear, Jake seemed uptight. He usually makes jokes and puts us all at ease."

"No need to worry, he was probably tired from moving, there was a fire at his house. Did you know?"

Phyllis voice was quieter, as if thinking, "Hmm. And where does Belinda come in on that?"

"I have no idea why you even mention her."

"They had dinner together; Our table was across from theirs. Belinda's quite a flirt."

"I guess that's good to know, but how is she with Abby?"

"Strange you would ask; she barely looks the child's way and never touches her."

"Maybe she has never been around a baby and doesn't know what to do with one."

"No, that's not it. I've been watching this all along. I believe she is one of those people who watch out for self and the rest of the world can be hanged."

"Good for her. I could use a bit of that."

"Yes, you could," Phyllis replied. "Have a good day, and come over when you can. Love you."

She no longer would be going to her mother's house after work each evening. Her mind was made up. It would hurt too much to know she no longer had the freedom to drop in there or at Jake's anytime she wanted to see Abby. It was time to close that chapter of her life and begin a new one.

Chapter
7

....

"What's going on, Hon?" Charles studied his daughter's reaction to the question. When she didn't reply, he continued, "you weren't in church, that would be about three weeks now and Jake seemed about as stressed out as the church mouse being chased by the cat, and now your momma tells me you don't drop by to see Abby and if a baby misses people she's pretty sure Abby misses you."

"Jake and I decided not to see each other. There was nothing there, anyway."

"I guess, on your part but there's a good man that's getting away. Belinda will be a lucky girl."

"That's good, isn't it?" She was searching for a new subject to their conversation when he said,

"Are you attending church anywhere?"

"Yes, Sir. It's good, except you and Mom aren't there."

෴

They were starting harvest the next week. The combine went out first, she and Dante thought the beans were ready, but along with harvest came the heavy dew. Dante stood with her, "It all looks so good," she said. "And it has come upon us much quicker than I thought possible."

Dante laughed, "Yes, Ma'am, once it starts turning it's definitely ready."

"You've done a good job, Dante.' Leading the men and seeing they finish jobs is a lot, isn't it? You are all going to feel it once you begin twelve-hour shifts." She glanced his way, "More?"

"He laughed, "I'd say sixteen, once we start harvest, we're fighting to stay above the rains."

"Yeah, rain. We prayed for it June and July, hoped for a little through August and now we want nothing to do with that heaven sent offering." They shared laughter. "We are pretty fickle."

"Yes, we are. Have you eaten?" Dante' was on his way to his truck. "I'm headed to the Corner."

"Is it still operating?" She had left her vehicle on the turn-row. "I had no idea. I guess they still have the fried bologna sandwiches, right?"

"You bet, but I'm going for the ham and cheese. If you're hungry, hop in. I'm buying."

"Actually, this walking has been effective. I'm hungry and out of snacks at the office."

"Hop in." He moved papers out of the passenger seat and she joined him. "They now have tables, if you remember, used to all you could do was order and stand," He grinned. "If you want to sit, we can do that."

"Why don't we play that by ear?" Within minutes she was glad, she'd said that. She hadn't expected to see Jake's truck at the Corner. She was told he went home for lunch each day. But her mother was the one relayed that information, saying, "he checks on Abby." When Dante asked what she would like and if she could find a table for them, she was more than happy to do so. "I think I'll skip the sandwich and just have something cold to drink," she said, eyeing a table in back of the room.

Someone put a nickel in the Juke box at front of the building and a slow dance song began to play.

"Poor Sucker," Dante remarked. "All the songs are old ones, but a few are still good. Do you dance?" He was opening a brown bag, and setting out two sandwiches. "Did you say you dance?"

"I used to try, but I seem to have two left feet. Do you?"

"Yeah, in my family, you'd be half dead if not able to move your feet. Why, they are probably dancing now, you know, street parties and music and selling stuff in between, you know, yard sales."

"You are Italian?" He waited as a young girl came and set two glasses of drink on the table.

"I'm a half-breed, or maybe a mutt. Who knows? But the name is Italian and my mother is, also. You should come with me some weekend and meet her. She is unique." He handed her one of the sandwiches. "You owe it to yourself to try this." He watched as she took a plastic knife from a table pack and halved it. "I dream of these sandwiches some nights when I can't sleep."

"Are you worrying, the reason you can't sleep, or, just can't sleep?"

"Both, probably, but any worry I have never measures up to others, like losing Terry."

"I know," she replied and they seemed to drift into remembering's territory.

Lunch break didn't last long and they were ready to head back to the farm, but in leaving they must walk past Jake and a few other farmers. Dante' smiled and exchanged a few words with them but Amanda found a way to side step confrontation and found a different path to the truck.

"You all right?" Dante asked, sliding into the driver's seat. "I lost you back there."

"Yeah, everything's fine." She stared out the side window, seeing Jake get in his truck.

"I wonder," Dante said, "Would you like to have a little Friday night fun? There's this dance and Karaoke every week and I've been wanting to go, but if you don't have a partner to dance…well, you get the picture?"

"Give me a minute," she said, "I've got to process this, I don't think I have anything." Truth was, she was so miserable at the moment, seeing Jake and none of the old comradery between them, she wanted to cry and what would that do? She couldn't understand her own emotions but one thing for certain, she wasn't doing anything to break the boredom or doldrums his absence caused.

"Yeah," she said, "I'd love to, as a friend, right? Nothing more, I've just come out of a jaded relationship and it behooves me," she did the italics thing on the word behooves, "To let that one settle in the dust, not that you aren't the perfect person to help a girl forget, handsome, companionable, and I can tell fun to be with and maybe not even interested in me…how does friendship and fun sound?"

"My thoughts, exactly." His grin confirmed the truth in his words.

"You want to know something? I wouldn't tell that to anyone, and haven't, go figure?"

"I'm honored, and some day when we have time, I'll give you a little of my history and gained wisdom." His laugh was catching. "I hope there's wisdom because there was pain."

She had not seen Jake get in his truck and for a minute pound the steering wheel in frustration, nor know Jake's dismay in seeing her with another man and she was smiling. That meant she was moving on. He wondered if she had prayed about their relationship, as, he had? But then it was his harsh words caused the rift, wasn't it? He made the call. He covered his hurt most times very well. Most times.

The night she accompanied Dante to the dance, was uneventful except she was a bit rusty, but they decided they would try another night when there was time, maybe a different place. Now that they were in full swing of harvest and the pickers going late hours, who knew when that would be.

How's the turn out?" She caught Woodsey at the turn row and climbed the ladder to ride a round or two with him. "It looks good."

Woodsey closed the door to the picker's cab. "Yeah, it's doing very well, but I believe it will get better once we clear where the water stood. I'm thinking there's a bit of land planeing needs to be done right in here, the water plus our machines making ruts to get the cotton planted didn't help us any."

"You and Dante make notes of these places and when harvest is over, we'll sit down together and decide what to do. I may be capable of getting jobs done, Woodsey, but I rely on you guys to tell me what's needed. I've got a lot to relearn here on flat land farming."

"How was it in North Carolina?"

"Well, one thing we found was cotton required a sandier type soil, if it was high in organic matter, it didn't do as well. Go figure. That's bound to play out, here, to an extent, too, isn't it? The guy making the documentary had no clue, he just wanted to shoot the story but leave out the story."

"I take it, that's the one set fire to Jake's home. He must be a real." Woodsey's face turned red. "I lost my word, there, sorry Amanda."

She giggled, as she always had with Woodsey. "I know what you almost said and yes, he was."

"Was it jealousy made him do something that extreme? He'll probably go to jail for that stunt."

"Don't count on it. His family's known for paying their way out of situations. Clark, has gotten out of a lot of things that way and I don't understand why he is so extreme. The one place he excels is in documentaries. He's brilliant."

"You sound sold on that character and that means you two are as different as daylight and dark."

"No." Amanda was emphatic. "I came here to leave all that behind. It's not that he followed me, but that he is working near here and drove over, but I was very clear that he and I have nothing between us."

Woodsey was making the turn at the end of the cotton rows, a deep drainage ditch bordering the turn. "Mandy, you may not see the implications in what that fellow has done, but I'm telling you, he's dangerous. If a man goes to one extreme to make a point, he's not finished, he will hound you to death."

"He becomes overbearing when he's drinking and thinks he is right, even when the rest of the world knows he isn't, but I don't think he would be that stupid, that he's dangerous."

"Mandy, that's even worse, the drinking part. Now you be careful, that fellow is dangerous and I'd guess he's evil. There won't always be someone around to save you like Jake was. You hear me?"

She was reading her devotional that night when the word evil came up. "Do not be envious of evil men, nor desire to be with them for their hearts devise violence and their lips talk of trouble. By wisdom a house is built and by understanding it is established; by knowledge the rooms are filled with precious and pleasant riches. A wise man is full of strength…" She placed her finger on the passage and sit higher on the pillows staring into space.

It was Jake she saw, as plain as if he stood before her. God had just shown her the difference in two men; Jake and Clark.

Before, she had been caught up in the world of creating documentaries, sitting up fake rooms that caught the eye of regular people while filled with expensive object priced beyond an ordinary budget; the elite had no budget, they bought what they wanted, except it seemed Clark was in the habit of going beyond his own means; purchasing and discarding items as though he was entitled, using his good looks to wheel and deal when often he had not a penny in his pocket, because he had spent it.

Turning off the light, she sank down into the covers. Tomorrow was a busy day. Dante' had explained there was a test plot with several varieties being harvested to see which performed best in the area farm's type of soil, and the company that provided the seed wanted to meet her. She had drifted off when she heard a noise at the back door. No animal could make that much noise. She started to dial Jake, when she remembered he was off limits, instead she dialed the police department and ask if anyone was patrolling the area and was told there was one they would notify to drive by her house.

It was twenty minutes later they called to say their fellow officer had shined the light on the back of the house and scared someone away. "There was a black sports car on the next street over, would you know anyone with that type of vehicle," they asked. She gave them Clark's name and they said they had released him on bond that morning.

She had gasp, allowing them to speculate she hadn't known he was in town nor their facility. "A week ago," she said, "But not last night."

"Ma'am, I'm not supposed to tell you this, but that man has an evil intent to do someone harm. If you know him, be extra careful. He made a lot of loose threats. Of course, he was drinking heavily and lost all stops as to what he thought." When she didn't reply, he asked, "Would you have a place you could stay until he moves out of this area? I understand he's working in the next town over."

She thanked him and went into the kitchen and pushed a chair under the door knob. As if that will help, she thought, but it made her feel better. With that in mind, she dragged one of the kitchen chairs to her bedroom, locked the door and pushed that chair under the door knob. In bed, she pulled the cover up to her ears and curled into a knot. What was Clark thinking? It was three in the morning when she changed the clock's alarm from five to seven. She was exhausted. If Clark was coming, he should have been there, but if he was drinking, he was sound asleep somewhere and her body was screaming for rest. If she didn't make it, tomorrow, Dante would go on without her...

What was that noise? She jumped out of bed; it must be the police; Clark was at the door and she was caught sleeping. But it wasn't the police or Clark, even if her body was in a jerking mode, more than shaking or trembling, and her nerves were on edge. It seemed an eternity until she had her body under control. This just wouldn't do. Lots of people exist on fewer hours sleep than she'd gotten. The clock said seven, Dante would be meeting the people in the South field. She brushed her teeth and slapped on a bit of sun screen protection, jumped into the jeans she'd laid out last night and grabbed her purse. She could be there in ten minutes if she combed her hair on the way, zipped her pants and buttoned her blouse. She could do this; jerky body movements and all.

Dante, ever gracious was serving the guests coffee from the shop kitchenette, as the men called it, a long wood table, man height, that held a coffee maker and components. Occasionally donuts were there. She was beginning to enjoy Dante as the man her dad first explained him to be. The man knew work and how to delegate to the employees and as she hoped he and Woodsey were friends. She heard of neighboring headquarters that were always bickering and she prayed, never here.

The day was long and the visiting brass from the research station were tedious in their task. She learned a thing or two and found their work impressive. It was geared toward making better seed, for different types of soil and in the end, they were the farmer's friend. She finally felt the tug of sleep and leaving the men, drove home thinking to take a nap before Dante arrived. They had become a twosome since not play an instrument. He was fun to be with and made no advances.

She stepped out of the shower to hear the phone. "Hey, Dad, how are you?"

"Was the day successful?" He was interested in the plots. "We started them in earnest, about five years ago. You remember? Well, I'm glad you made it. I was in the coffee shop and heard you had a bit of excitement last night. Are you okay?" He listened to her rendition and cautioned before hanging up. "Amanda, men are crazy when they don't get their way, be it in business or their private life, that's the renegades who don't value another man's rights." She knew he was right.

"You already know which this man is, so be careful. I'm afraid he's already shown his true colors and you have to realize he does not mean good toward you. Don't think you can handle this situation, he's coming to your home in darkness, that means he is a man with dark feelings in his heart and there's no good will there. Be on guard."

For some reason she felt a shudder go through her body as she closed the cell phone. She knew Clark was trouble but could it be the drinking had progressed to the point he was that dark figure the police and her dad painted? She tried to call the one person of the crew she could count on to tell her the truth. "Polly, thanks for answering. Can you tell me, what's going on in Clark? He tried to break in to my house last night and the Police are on alert about him." She listened. "You mean he's jeopardizing the documentary? You saw how he demonized me. That's why I left but that's so far out. You mean he is blaming me for leaving and it's my fault this documentary isn't going well? That's ridiculous. He's the director, I only sit up the backdrop for the scenes and I'm not in this one."

She lay down, all the while trying to process what Polly had told her. Maybe it was his conscience, the little boy who looked just like him had to play heavy on his mind. For what she'd seen of the woman, she loved her son, she just needed financial help in raising him. If Clark's parents found out they had a grandson, surely, they would lend support. It would be only a dip in the bucket they would be sharing, but if the mother feared they would take her son and raise him as they had Clark, that's where the real worry lay. The handsome little boy led her to think of Abby. She tried to push missing Abby out of her thoughts on a daily basis but it was impossible; the ache in her heart for Abby and Jake was like a needle pushing its way through her body and hurt more than she wanted anyone to know.

When she awakened a light rain was falling, the men would go home early. Most had felt the heat and considered it a long week. They needed to spend time with family. Dante did not mention family.

Chapter

8

....

"Look at you." Dante was one to appreciate all things beautiful. "You are breath taking. What happened? When you left you were about as wilted as a piece of lettuce, but here you are. What magic pill did you take?"

"I love your festive outlook, Sir. That, along with my hour's nap, should take me to ten o'clock, when no doubt I'll turn into a rock, or is that a frog?"

"The frog bit will be me," he said as he opened the door to the truck. "Sorry, it's the farm truck, when your dad set me up with a truck at my disposal, I let my vehicle go, no need paying insurance on something that just sits there."

"I understand, completely. So, did you get a nap? The heat and the reps were pretty stressful."

"Grueling is the word. I think you and your dad run Fair Acres in a more laid-back way." Once he was behind the wheel, he added, "I need to ask if it's okay with you we hire Woodsey's son on a full-time basis for the rest of the fall. We need a person to go behind us and keep things in order."

"Can he, do it? He's young."

"He filled in for Woodsey during his wife's surgery and did a great job during planting season."

"Planting and harvest show the true grit of a person, don't they?" Woodsey and her father's caution concerning Clark came to mind. "I didn't get a chance to ask about Woodsey's wife the other day when he was reading me the riot act about being careful."

"About that guy?"

"Yeah."

"Want to talk about it?"

"No." She gave a sort of laugh as he shrugged. "But I will. They, meaning my dad and Woodsey think he would hurt me. Clark loses control when he drinks. The alcohol takes over and he doesn't think straight. I believe, at those times he wants to talk, thinking he can sway my judgement, but I'm through talking and what Clark can't have becomes an obsession."

"This is the guy who tried to break into your home? The one Jake tied to the porch post?"

"Yeah, the neighbors must think I'm a scarlet lady."

"What happened to you and Jake? One day it was you, him and baby and then he's gone. Let's face it, Jake was stopping by to see you and we all got a kick out of seeing him excited, but we couldn't see you and I guess we just wondered what happened?"

"I don't know what happened. Evidently, it wasn't meant to be. I don't think we know."

"Do you miss him?"

"Yeah."

They arrived but before leaving the truck he turned to her. "Just to warn you, I'm singing tonight."

He opened the door and came around to her side. "Didn't want to alarm or embarrass you."

"I can't wait." She smiled taking his hand. "Shouldn't you be escorting someone else?"

"Are you kidding? No one holds a candle to you. Be careful, grass is a bit wet from the shower."

Jake arrived in time to see Dante opening the door and a woman stepping down. Interesting, he thought, but when she turned and it was Amanda, his heart did a flip. He didn't know if it was good, he was here, tonight, or not. Phyllis had prevailed. He couldn't know his *countenance* as she called it looked so down, "leave Abby with me tonight and go out and have a good time, Jake. You are showing the wear and tear of too much time as a parent and not any as a young man." She insisted and he finally gave in. Where did one go? It was no fun going to the movies alone. He could do that at home. He called Belinda and asked what she was doing. She replied, singing at the Net. Here he was and there was Amanda. Something inside pushed up, resentment that she was with another man, or his determination she would not cloud his thinking. She seemed to be faring very well, then why wasn't he? She was in his every thought right along with Abby. He loved two women, one out of his reach, the other a fingertip away and he was trying to love a third, but that wasn't working.

The Net was a surprise to Amanda, she had actually offered her advice as to the décor of the building. That was five years past, when she heard they were running an ad for the general public's interest in naming the establishment and how to bring precedence to the name. Phyllis had sent her the brochure and, on a lark, Amanda mailed in her suggestions with full blown illustrations. She had signed her name as Amanda Leigh. She had left off Lanis and not given a return address, in case the whole thing went wrong under someone else direction.

Now, as she stood in the foyer, the whole thing seemed so familiar, it had taken a moment to realize this was her design and it was very effective. The whole theme had been to draw people in. The ceiling was black fish net draped from corner to corner with small lights near the ceiling that would cast onto the net giving them an ethereal almost star in the sky look. Two canoes were suspended, one over the bar area, the other near the rest rooms and the whole atmosphere of beech wood and stark black table tops circling the dance floor were as effective as she had hoped.

Dante saw her admiration. "It's stunning, isn't it? The owner said they were never successful in contacting the designer and that little item lies dormant on the block until whoever it is comes forth." He had seen it all before, but tonight all the lights were on because the rain had brought out enough it was a full house. He waited for the full impact to hit her, thinking she seemed pleased with the whole atmosphere.

Finally, she said, "I like it. All in all, it's pretty grand."

"Come with me," he said, "I'll show you the rest of the place and where the restrooms are located, in case I'm away from you longer than expected, when I sing." She followed as he showed her the dining room for private bookings and the kitchen with a full range of silver appliances and then the *warm up room for the musicians and the dais, she had specially designed to showcase the one* entertaining. But Of course, he wouldn't know that. "Can you make your way back," he asked. "I need to give them the music to the rendition of the song I'm singing, and I'll join you in just a few."

While on the grand tour the lights had been lowered and most of the tables were occupied, she saw one table almost to the back with a lone person and decided to see if the other seats were available. She leaned over to speak above the drum roll into his ear, "Pardon, me, are you saving the remaining seats?" She felt rather than saw the man's head shaking that he wasn't saving them, as the music came across loud, she sit in the nearest empty chair. "Thank you," she hollered across the table as another woman bent to kiss the man and took the seat beside him.

Someone turned on the huge ceiling fans and for one moment she caught the fragrance of a man's aftershave and it reminded her of Jake and the first time she met him, but there must be a hundred men in the room who wore the same fragrance. The two had their heads together and seeing Dante across the room where strobe lights revealed more faces, she stood to find her way over to where he was pointing to an empty table. "I think the couple that was sitting here are out on the dance floor," she said. To which he replied, "I know them, they said we could barge in. They don't care, they've been married a year now." He laughed. "I wasn't sure you knew who you were sitting by."

"I guess not, who was it?" He was pointing across the room and as the strobe lights circled, she saw Jake and wondered if the woman who kissed him was Belinda. Evidently, Jake had no idea she was that close to him. She turned her attention to Dante. "That would have been embarrassing."

"No reason, ever, for you to be embarrassed. It is what it is. Life goes on. Right?" He pulled the chair out from the table and waited for her to be seated. "Have you met Belinda?" She shook her head, no. "Take my word for it, that is no great loss. She returns ever so many years, I've been told, when one marriage has ended and she is looking for the next candidate."

"I didn't think she ever married." Amanda remembered asking Phyllis if she was single or divorced and Phyllis replied, as she understood, Belinda had been away working on her career with no time for matrimony and that most folks speculated she was waiting until Jake decided to settle down. "Would Jake know if she was once married?"

"The only reason I know," Dante replied, "Is because a buddy of mine came so close, but found out about the others. He lives in the city and has no family from our little southern town."

"Others as in plural?" Dante nodded. "That sounds almost like the black widow story, I know a man she needs to meet." Amanda shook her head. "By now he should be long gone. Didn't I read in the paper that the people doing the documentary had left and were returning to California?"

"That sounds right. The article said they came here from doing a documentary in North Carolina, But are we talking about the same man we've discussed before?" When she shook her head yes, Dante burst out laughing. "That would be a match, I'm thinking." The band music dropped low as the leader stepped to the center of the dais and the couples dancing took their seats. Dante's friends joined them as Dante did the introductions. "Amanda Lanis meet Gary and Laurie Stover."

"It's Karaoke time," came over the speaker, "and to start out, ladies first, Miss Belinda Miles." Everyone was giving a round of applause as she rose from sitting by Jake and placed a kiss on his cheek. There was more applause and a few cat calls, overpowered by whistles as she stepped on to the platform. "Miss Belinda will be singing an old Patsy Cline favorite."

As the band played the words drift over the heads of those dancing, "please accept my apology." Dante offered her his hand and they were out on the dance floor. "I'm a little rusty," she said, but he just laughed and pulled her close.

So, the evening went and then it was time for Dante. The crowd must have heard him sing before because they went wild, calling his name and stomping the floor. Amanda was prepared to enjoy whatever song he chose and she was not disappointed, "Remember when," Dante held the full room of people's attention and when he finished different people were calling out other songs. She was so captured by what he was capable of, she didn't at first register someone was tapping on her shoulder. "Amanda?" That got her attention. She turned to find Jake standing with his hand out. "May I have this dance?" She glanced toward the table where he had been sitting with Belinda. "She had to leave. She only came to sing as they had asked, earlier in the week."

Dante was singing A Love Like Ours and Jake was leading her onto the dance floor. She tried to hear Dante above the thudding of her heart or was it Jake's? She wasn't certain, only that they were in step as though they had danced together all the of their lives and she had thought she and Dante did well. "How have you been?" He asked. "Fine," she replied, "you?" He said, "Busy. Before the song ends, Amanda, Abby misses you." She thought on that. "How would you know?" He glanced down, his heart in his eyes and his voice husky as he spoke, "Come by, Amanda, drop in to see her. I think you will know." She couldn't resist, "Aren't you afraid of what someone like Baumgarten might think about me?"

Jake's body seemed to droop, "Maybe so, but I'll chance it. Just come by." It was at that moment someone hit Jake and he went reeling into an empty table at the edge of the dance floor, leaving Amanda standing alone and confused as to what had happened.

From his position on the raised dais, Dante saw the commotion and was by her side immediately. By now, Clark had his hands on her shoulders, screaming down into her face. "You caused it all, you cheap…" That was when Dante and Jake overpowered him, dragging him toward the double doors of the Net. Clark continued to scream obscenities toward Amanda as she followed trying to find what had caused this public assault. She knew the police would arrive any minute. It was the last name he called Amanda, she wasn't sure what happened, or whether it was Jake or Dante that hit Clark and knocked him out. Someone hollered, "there's three Police cars barreling down the road."

She was standing with her hands to her face when Dante found her a minute later. "Come, let me take you home." It was as though her voice was gone. She pointed to where a crowd surround the truck, they arrived in. "Whaaat?" Dante couldn't believe what he was seeing. "He must have seen us drive in and waited until we were inside and then waited again until I was singing which left you alone."

Jake finished speaking with the Police. He knew the men. "What's going on?" He asked as the crowd drew his attention. "Is that what you are driving? What you were driving?"

Dante said, "Jake, could you take Amanda home? I'll have to report this destruction to the police in order for the Insurance to pay for the damage." She started to protest but the two men gave each other a quick glance and Jake had a hand on her elbow and was already guiding her to where he had parked. They walked past someone from the Net, working over a revised Clark, revised enough to hurl yet another insult her direction.

"I was coming after you, Bitch," he screamed. "I'm not done. You might as well look behind every bush. When you least expect it, I'll have my hand around your throat."

Stunned, Amanda stepped closer. "What have I done to you, Clark? Stop this before someone gets hurt."

Clark winced but managed to laugh at her words. "You're the one will get hurt. I promise."

She would have said more, but Jake was propelling her toward his truck, now. "Give it up, Amanda. The man's so drunk he doesn't know what he's saying, and probably not what he's done. This must be a second offense and they will throw him in jail."

"Third," she said. Jake stopped walking to look down into her face. "He was here again last week and the Police detained him, but I thought by now he had started back to California."

"Not North Carolina?" They were a few steps from the truck.

"No, that was the last documentary. A friend told me after being here they were to return for an assignment in California. That's where the company is located."

"Why is he upset with you, or blame you for whatever is troubling him?" Jake opened the truck door.

"Evidently, you don't say no to Clark." She climbed up and slid onto the seat.

"But you did?" He wasn't about to ask why and she wasn't willing to explain.

"Have you had anything to eat?"

"I'm not hungry."

"That's not what I ask." He pulled out onto the highway, heading toward his home.

"This is not the direction to my house."

"No, it's not." His voice was low with the inflection of a stubborn man's *don't argue with me tone*.

In minutes she saw the lights to his home. She noticed the excavator was gone and the new drive was in. "If my mother is there, I don't want to see her."

"You won't. Just hang tight. I'm parking in the back. Your mother always parks in the front and she leaves quickly." He turned the lights off and went in, and as he said her mother left soon after. She sit, until he knocked on the window and said, "Amanda, don't be stubborn, please, come inside."

If emotions could be in conflict, hers were. On one hand, she had just dealt with one man who thought he knew what was best for her and here was another. On the other hand, she wanted to see Abby so desperately, had he not asked, she would have stood at the window looking in. She was that torn but he opened the door and with his hand firm upon her arm, walked her inside, while she wondered, after seeing Abby how was she to get home?

Expecting to find Abby asleep, she was elated to see her in a little swing in full motion, her feet touching the floor. "Ahh, Abby, my little darling, what are you doing? Look at you, how you've grown." She turned to Jake. "Why is she awake?"

"I don't know, your mother thinks it's because my hours are late and she waits up for me."

"Every night?"

"Just about." He grinned when Abby stopped the swing from moving and was straining toward him to pick her up. "How's my baby?"

"But you aren't in the field, tonight. How did you talk my mom into staying over?"

"It was her idea. She said I was looking a bit worn around the edges. Did she know you would be there?"

"No." His eyebrows raised, as if questioning her reply. "You don't believe me?"

He shrugged and took the rocking chair. "Take that chair. I'd offer you this one but we do this every night. She's gotten used to it. Talk to her."

Taking a little cloth giraffe from the table, Amanda begin, "what have you been doing? All dressed up in your jammies and wide awake. I thought you would be asleep." Abby was so still, her eyes wide, listening, as if deciding she knew that voice and then her arms went up and she leaned toward Amanda. "I believe she remembers me," Amanda whispered. "How could that be?" Jake wanted to say. "I know why," instead he said, "if you'll take her, I'll go shower and then we will drive you home."

Chapter
8

....

She wanted to call Dante when she was home and ask what happened with Clark, but as she checked the time on the clock it was too late. What would the police have done with Clark. She couldn't understand why he hadn't left with the crew. It was a shock to see him at the Net. If he had a problem with her leaving the job, Clark knew it was because of him and any perks that would have come her way were automatically transferred to his account and Clark liked living the high life.

Seeing Abby had eased the apprehension she felt over Clark but now there was the situation with Jake. True, he had not spoken of their past acquaintance. Other than his plea that she not be a stranger to Abby he was withdrawn, leaving them alone until it was time to drive her home.

She jumped when the phone rang. She was that deep in thought, nothing made sense and she didn't know what to expect from this point on. She picked up the phone, carefully, but it was Dante.

"Hey, pretty boss lady. Is it too late to fill you in on what happened after you left?"

"I'm so happy to hear your voice. Tell me what happened, to everyone and everything."

"All right, people first. Your friend who acts like an enemy, is in jail. Sleeping it off, I might add. The truck, has a few problems and each one requires fixing. We'll check our surplus tomorrow to see if there's anything to work with. I was able to drive it back. I hate that it happened and ask you to forgive my sending you home with Jake, but it would have worn you out staying through all that."

"It was uncalled for. I don't suppose he explained what set him off or why he showed up at the Net."

"Nope, cursed your name on a regular basis, and," Dante quit talking as if thinking, and then he said, "He gave our police boys to understand he wouldn't be finished until you were properly punished."

"I suppose he said until I'm dead." She sighed. "I promise you I've done nothing to deserve that."

"I never believed for a minute that you did." He was quiet again. "I don't suppose you ever turned him down over anything?"

"Fraid so, lots of times."

"A drinking man doesn't have a lick of sense, Amanda. He dwells on the injustice he believes he received and usually turns into a raving lunatic."

"He did seem to evolve that way on the last while we were working together, but when I first met him, he was almost perfect."

"I'm trying not to overstep my bounds, Amanda, but…do you two have a child? He kept saying the little boy and that bitch of a woman and we couldn't tell who he was talking about. And when they ask who he meant he said you. They questioned him thoroughly. I'd be afraid for my future if I were you."

"Oh, that makes me sick to my stomach. I don't have a child and I've never been to bed with that jerk. Please excuse the honesty. The child is with his first wife and that's the reason I turned down marriage to Clark, he kept her a secret until by accident I met them. So, since we're friends, because I know Jake will hear and think the worst of me, I want to tell you, I do love Abby, Terry and Amy Lou's little girl, as for Clark's denial of having a child, that precious little boy looks just like his daddy. Clark can't deny him and the sad part is the mother and the little boy need him in the worst way."

"Why would he imply it's you that he's going to punish?"

"I don't know. A friend said he has become radical and I should be careful. That is a hard task."

"Would you say he is stalking you?"

"If he lived closer, there would probably be more times, but with him living a distance away," she was thinking out loud, "he has been around this last month enough…" She paused, "yes, I hadn't thought about it but yes, I guess he is."

"Then," said Dante, "you must be extra careful where you go. He seems crazed, Amanda? Is he on drugs, too? Maybe he has been all along but something's eating away at him presently and let's say he may be relying on the drugs more and they are not his best friend."

"Dante," she said, "I honestly don't know but that does seem reasonable, doesn't it?"

"He's in jail tonight, so get to bed and get a good night's sleep." They may let him out tomorrow."

She felt helpless with what was happening. It was the busiest time of the year for Clark to be harassing her. It made her wonder if he had lost his job. Why would he still be here when the others had left?

What was she to do? She loved being in her home. Even if it was at her parents, she felt restricted.

They would welcome her but she wasn't ready to go back. Still, it made her shudder to think Clark would hurt her. Just in case, she needed to accept the inevitable, at least in her head, if not in her heart.

Woodsey popped into her office the next morning. "You okay?" She hesitated, too long for Woodsey. "Mandy, I heard the story. Town's a buzzin' and they still got that other culprit in jail but Mandy, I found out who he is. Do you know his history?"

"Clark? Only what he told me and I did meet his parents once. Wait, I don't underst…"

"It ain't a good story. His brother died young and this one, you know, was left and he never got over It, but maybe that's because as the story goes, his mother was awful hard on him and maybe even implied he was responsible for the younger one dying. That would be a terrible guilt on a young'un. But," Woodsey held up one hand, "Before you feel too sorry for him, think of all the pain he inflicts and what if there's truth in the other part of the story? That possibly, he was responsible for the young one's death, maybe resentment he got a younger one's attention, don't the young one's normally get more attention? I ain't sayin I believe it but I am saying I don't know the truth but we gotta keep a sane mind here and not throw out such, because we gotta stay safe and keep our family safe, you know that."

He was studying her, more of a scrutiny, as he tried to figure out what she knew. "There was this fellow sent in here to warn you, but he didn't, did he? He went on back to his place, said he prayed for you, but the Lord knew he couldn't do what he was supposed to. Somehow, he was tied to your fellow, Clark."

"What was he supposed to do? Kill me?" She didn't like Woodsey's expression. And then it hit her what he said, "What do you mean? You heard the family sent someone to warn me?" Fear raced through her mind. "How would you know that, Woodsey?"

"No one else knows, Mandy. I was alone at the shop, working on that old piece we put on the back of the tractor to pick up used poly pipe and I heard the door open but I thought it was just the wind. Next thing I know there's something hard poked middle my back. I say, I ain't got no money, you just as well move on. I thought it was a joke. You know, one of our men. This voice says, "where's the boss lady. She's not in her office." Honest to goodness, I'm still processing it and even went home thinkin about it, but then I felt scared down to my toes when I woke up middle of night and it hit me there was no one would know the things that man knew. At the time, I thought, Boy, one of our guys is makin up a bag of baloney. I was sweatin bullets and wanted to call you in the middle of the night but I thought what if this is a joke, on me, and you are asleep in your bed. Then I call Jake to kind of feel how the wind's stirrin on this and he tells me that Clark guy was at the Net and got put in jail again and I say to myself, then who's this joker tellin me that cockeyed story, the one said that Benson guy is dangerous?"

All she could do was stare at Woodsey. "They're going to let him out today, aren't they? Help me, Woodsey, can you remember if the person did come from family or if someone else got in on the story and they are playing you in order to get to me?"

Woodsey thought it through. "It seemed when he started out, he said Clark's a rich boy, used to getting his way. They sent me, the fellow said, when he wasn't checking in with family and they said he must be doing something we aren't aware of." Woodsey shook his head, "I don't know, Mandy. Maybe you better go stay at your dad's. This seems like your friend's got a mental problem and the man didn't say exactly, but he implied that your Clark fellow gets on drugs and doesn't watch when he uses them."

"I feel bad about him, Woodsey, there had to have been a deep-rooted problem with Clark if the family keeps tabs on him. I don't understand why he decided I was the cause of everything, I'm not."

"You can't afford to start feelin' sorry for this fellow, Mandy. He said he was going to kill you."

Even with Woodsey's concern, Amanda decided Clark would be gone and she was going to sleep in her own bed. Surely, she could take advantage of the one night he would be farthest away.

It was ten o'clock when the Police called, and she agreed to go down to the station. When she arrived, she was escorted into the captain's office. She thought it a bit strange an old clipboard lay on his desk. "I'm set in my ways, I guess. We do use computer print outs." He put the clipboard aside.

"Miss Lanis?" She nodded. "We ask you to come in that we might get your take on Clark Benson. You may have heard, he was released this morning and told to return to his home where we understand his family does keep tabs on him."

"Do you mean they try to be aware of where he is daily or they watch him by the hour?"

"Does it concern you, Miss Lanis, whether someone keeps tabs on Mr. Benson?"

"Wouldn't you be concerned? In the beginning I thought of it as Clark's temper but then I begin to hear he was making threats to kill me. It is very concerning. What should I do?"

"It is not good to spend nights alone, if you could stay with your parents. One other time we thought Mr. Benson miles away and he hid out here. That night he tried to enter your house. You called and asked if we had a car patrolling your area and we had to pick him up." He made an entry on the clipboard. "We need to know your thoughts on the times Mr. Benson has returned to your home and more important, do you think he would hurt you?"

She had thought on this, and knew she wanted to reject her own conclusion. "Yes, he would."

∞

Phyllis checked to be sure little Abby was sleeping. Her heart was heavy. Clair Baily sent a text early that morning. "Phyllis, I know you must be worn out with worry over this man stalking your daughter. It is all abuzz in town but I don't know if it made the news. Any way you are both in my prayers. I don't have time to talk as I'm driving to my appointment." She was glad Clair didn't have time to talk but by the time several hours passed, she could wait no longer. She sit in the rocker and called Charles. Unknown to Phyllis, it was one o'clock when Jake returned for a long-sleeved shirt, he needed in doing a job of hand spraying. He heard Amanda's name mentioned and stood listening from the kitchen. He could only hear one side of the conversation and had to fill in the blanks.

"Charles, do you know about Amanda being stalked? Clair says it's all over town that our daughter is being stalked by God only knows who because she hasn't told me. Do you know anything about this?" There was a silence and then Phyllis said, "That's all well and good that you think she doesn't want to worry us, but...well, I'm worried. We are her parents. Can you talk to her? She might listen to reason, coming from you." Again, there was silence and then Phyllis was getting out of the chair. Jake closed the door quietly as he left but he was almost to the shop when he realized he left his phone. Phyllis was still talking to Charles when he returned. "No, Charles. I believe it happened this week."

She closed the cell, disgruntled that neither she nor Charles had been informed, but Amanda was a grown woman. Still, she needed to ask someone questions that might have heard more. Maybe it was Jake. She found him in the kitchen. "Jake, Amanda is being stalked. Do you know about it?"

Jake leaned against the counter where his mother used to fold clothes fresh from the dryer. "I'm not sure anyone told me she was being stalked, Phyllis. But I was at the Net, the other night when that guy she worked with was there and yes, Benson showed out."

121

"Was it bad and was his problem, which I don't know anything about this, but was it directed at my daughter, alone?"

Jake rubbed his chin; he hadn't shaved that morning. "I can't say it was, as he gave me a mighty push into a row of empty tables. No one knew what that was about, except we were dancing."

"Are you seeing Amanda, socially?"

"If you're asking did I invite her on a date, no, ma'am, I am not seeing her socially, but I'd like to."

"For heaven's sakes, then, Jake, why not?"

She was so intent, he found himself laughing and after looking bewildered, she joined in. "Well, why not?" She doubled in laughter. "I'm sorry. This all comes as a shock and I'm not laughing about it, because it is no laughing matter. Maybe my nerves are on edge. You ever have that problem?" She gained control and said, "With my and Charles history, it's no wonder she doesn't confide." Jake was not laughing now. "Clair text me early this morning that the whole town knows she is being stalked. That worries me. She could be hurt, kidnapped, killed. I don't know if Amanda would consider such could happen to her. You may not know how stubbornly independent my daughter is."

Jake held up a hand in order to speak. "I made a huge mistake. I didn't tell her of an incident concerning her honor and that's what estranged us from each other."

"I wondered about that." Phyllis eyed him as a bird would a worm. "Was it that serious you couldn't share with her?"

"It was our favorite deacon, cornered me and told me he was aware she was sleeping with me, which she wasn't, never has, and he further said, our church doesn't need loose women like that. I couldn't reason with the man that his story was far from truth. I was meeting with my insurance agent shortly after that and I said something that hurt her feelings and I didn't go into it to explain why and not only did she quit me, she quit Abby and I know she loves Abby. So, my feeble thought if she knew about our deacon, she would not attend our church, I didn't tell her, not knowing she had already made up her mind."

There were tears in Phyllis eyes. "That's my girl. Women are stubborn in my family." She blew out a deep breath. "I'm not sure when this happened but what can we do, I mean, myself, of course, what can be done to protect her? You feel sure this person will return?"

"Based on the fact, he has found her two times, now that the police have been involved, doesn't it stand to reason he will come back a third? For some reason I feel strongly that he will."

"I have an idea," said her mother. "What if we play on her genuine love for Abby. Because you need to be spraying, she will offer to keep Abby and you will know where she is. I can't help but wonder why they didn't suggest she stay with family because this could go either way." Jake didn't reply. "I get it," Phyllis said, nodding. "You think they did but knowing Amanda…"

∽∞∾

That night, the wind brought a change of temperature and it was said it was raining the next state.

It didn't matter what others thought. Amanda holed up in the office, until near eight o'clock the next morning and then drove into town. Family always had an opinion. She and Jake had reached an impasse. She couldn't bother Dante. He was running the farm. True, she went out each day to see how the operation was progressing. You could not fault men that were giving their all, working into the late hours of the night because it was the hurricanes down south always brought rain to the central states. High wind could take the locks of cotton right out of the boll. True, they were careful in the process of eliminating the green leaves to make the bolls open, but they could not out guess the weather.

She thought she was strong but last night proved otherwise. When she heard the glass breaking from the kitchen window, she had almost lost it. She decided upon viewing; the wind had thrown the old wooden chair through, causing the damage. Early this morning, she was first at the store, sitting slumped in the seat of the vehicle, watching when the lights went on and the employee unlocked the door. She prayed no one saw her hurrying to the sports section and certainly not to the glassed case where guns were locked safely away, but on display.

It had taken an hour to research the gun she wanted. It had to do the job if she was attacked but it also must fit in her purse. "You will have to go

123

to the County Seat and register," the man behind the counter said, "if you want it today or you can wait three days; nothing personal, it's the law. I cannot give it to you now, not until you have the correct papers." She had driven the eight miles, met the requirements and returned to collect the gun. Everything was a two- step procedure. Everything she did these days was in a hurry to get back to the farm. She couldn't let the employees who were conscientious with time see her dawdling about but the problem with Clark was ever on her mind.

Everything seemed to be falling into place. She accepted the package and was on her way out when she felt the tap on her shoulder and turned to face the man who sold her the gun. His expression was grave, to say the least. "Miss, don't ever point a gun at a person, no matter how bad they are, unless you have the guts to use it, or they might take it away from you and kill you."

"I know." He studied her for a moment, reluctant to let her go. She didn't blink. "I can do it."

The second item on her list was to have the glass in the window replaced. She had found part of an old tarp in the farm shop and taken it home to replace the blanket she'd managed to wrap to the frame of the screen that had been ripped away. It was dirty but the tarp would be water proof to a point if no one could manage the repair immediately. When the wind blew the chair into the glass it had shattered all over the wood porch. Examining the door, she muttered, "it's a wonder it didn't get you, too." There were places at the bottom as though someone in the past tried kicking it in. She shook her head and considered the job done. Pleased that she could handle it without calling on anyone, she went in to sit a few minutes and found the phone ringing.

"Miss Lanis?" The voice seemed anxious but familiar. "This is Captain Down. I talked with you last week, concerning your acquaintance, Clark Benson? I thought you should know, your neighbor called in a report of someone in the back area of your residence. She said it looked as though the person was breaking into your home by the back window or door and we sent a car down but he's a rookie and was delighted to go on call. He had lights flashing and siren going and scared the intruder away."

"When was this?" She drew a deep breath. "I can't believe you didn't call me."

"Miss Lanis. Have you checked your phone? We did, just as your neighbor said she tried, but there was no answer. Ma'am, we need for you to have our number in your phone, in case you ever need us." Amanda realized she had been so tired and slept so deep she had not heard the phone. "Ma'am, is everything all right?" She let the phone slip from her fingers. It wasn't the wind that shattered the window and the marks on the lower part of the door had probably happened while she slept.

She didn't tell anyone. Why would she bring another person in to what could be a death trap? Jake had called and said he was doing hand spraying in places the weeds were taking over. It was a perfect conversation to ask if she could keep Abby. She missed Abby in her arms. Before they realized, Abby would go through all the stages and rather be on her own moving around than encumbered by those who wanted to hold her. To keep her own business private, she forfeit holding Abby. She felt Jake's disappointment she hadn't offered to keep his daughter but every move she made toward Abby left her loving the child more while the heartache that someone else would one day be Abby's mother left her on the brink of despair and crying. No, she wouldn't let anyone see that side of her.

Work was brightened by the progress of the machines moving across the fields and the round bales spewed out to line the turnrows in waiting to be picked up and moved to the ginning facility. She watched, thinking the men were efficient as any trained person she had ever met. They all worked with one eye to the sky, praying it didn't rain or come a heavy wind storm that would blow the cotton from the boll. Harvest was as exciting and tiring as she remembered.

She was beginning to relax. Every night she propped the kitchen chair under the knob of the back door and then laid the gun on the night stand. The next afternoon when she stopped by to see her mother, Phyllis asked, "Amanda, did you buy a gun?"

"Why would you ask something so direct, Mother?" She had arrived after her mother came home from keeping Abby at Jakes. Now, she paused from laying silverware for the two of them on the table.

"Why wouldn't I? Caroline Page saw you in the sports section and she said if she was not mistaken you were purchasing a gun. Did you buy a gun?

"Yes, I did."

"Do you know how to use it?"

Completely mystified, Amanda watched her mother turning salmon cakes in a skillet. "I thought you would say, why would you do that or don't drop it and hurt yourself."

"Evidently, it's too late for that, so, do you know how to use it? You feel you might have to, so?"

"Just when I think I know you, Mother, you amaze me."

Phyllis chuckled. "Praise God for that, I figured you'd tell me to mind my own business."

"I'm not as skilled in the use as I would like to be."

"Can you get away an hour or so tomorrow evening?"

"Why?"

"I can teach you a little bit about your gun."

"Really, Mom?" Amanda practically leaned forward in surprise. "I'd love that."

"Soon as Jake gets home. Let's meet on the back of our farm where that big hump of dirt is."

"I can do that, but I'm surprised, let me rephrase that, you surprise me…you are something else."

"I hope that is a compliment," Phyllis gave a dry reply. "I often wonder if there's hidden meaning."

She was almost too tired after a day riding turn rows, with Dante to decide which field to move into next, but she had promised to meet her mother. "Don't forget," Phyllis mentioned. "Just a few reminders here and there could save your life. You told me this fellow was a big guy, so you have to be careful." Looking down the road and waiting, she sank deeper into the seat to be awakened later by someone pecking on the window.

"Hey, aren't you getting a little warm in there with the window rolled up?"

It was Jake. She had to get her bearings and wipe the drool off the corners of her mouth. "What are you doing here?"

"Your Mom said you would be here." He glanced across at the large pile of dirt from the last cleaning of the ditch. "She took Abby home with her." He grinned. "In fact, this will be Abby's first sleep over, not that she will remember much of it, but your mom said to tell you, there's weather coming in because that bunion on her foot is giving her fits." He shrugged. "She sent me to show you a few things about your gun. You have it with you, don't you?"

"Is this a set-up? She was fine last night. I don't suppose you saw the bunion in question?

He blew out a big breath, "I can leave, but as a matter of fact, she was wearing a house shoe and if a bunion is that large red ball on the side of her big toe, kind of sorta, yeah, I saw it. Red. She says throbbing." He shrugged and held up his hands. "Don't shoot the messenger."

A bit dubious, Amanda collected the gun and ammunition. "I'm so tired, we can skip this if you want."

"It's not what I want. If you feel there's a reason to know a little about a weapon, then let's do it."

"How is it that you are off early?" She glanced at the watch on her wrist. "Seven thirty."

"I'm second shift. I start at midnight, so I told her I'd run down and tell you why she's not here and since I am, let's see what you know."

"Not much," she admitted, "but I couldn't tell mother that."

They practiced an hour, until he noticed she was practically dragging her feet. "Come on, let's give it up. Go home with me and then you can go your way and I'll catch a few winks, but Miss Grace sent over a pot of soup and with a nip in the night air, I bet it will taste really good."

She tried to stifle a yawn. "I won't last long, but Miss Grace's cooking sounds just right for tonight."

She followed him home and they washed up together and then stood looking at the table; complete with a crockpot full of Soup, the bowls, glasses and silverware ready for use. "You and your women."

He held her hand and said grace. "What do you mean, my women?" He was dipping soup into her bowl. "I barely make it to church on time with the men working, but Miss Grace always brings food."

"I ate with Mother last night, you tonight and I'll be buying elastic waist pants, next."

"That would be a good Christmas present, right?" He saw her wrinkle her nose. "Is that a distasteful subject?"

"I haven't had a wonderful Christmas since the year mother and dad got a divorce."

"Then let us talk of something different," he said. "Weather? Taxes? Nothing?"

She was glancing around as if looking for something or someone and whether she was too tired to watch her words or simply wanted to know, even she would later wonder that she asked the question, "How are you and Belinda? Does she like soup?"

Jake began to laugh. "Are you asleep?"

"Why?" Her eyes flashed and then closed the lashes touching her cheeks. "I don't know what I said."

"I didn't think so." Mischief was in his smile. "So, how are you and Clark, the wonder man?"

"Who is that?"

"Amanda?" He laid down the spoon, leaned across to wave a hand in front of her eyes. "I can't believe this. Are you asleep?" She continued in a somewhat uncanny way to hit her mouth, not missing a beat as she emptied the bowl of soup. Finished, he cleared the table, led her to the sofa and went in to take his bath. He could not let her drive in that shape. After his bath, dressed in an old jogging suit, he settled in the recliner to decide what should be done about taking her home.

It was just before midnight when he awakened to the new guy on the picker telling him it was raining, they had shut down, secured everything and going in. He wasn't needed. There was the sound of someone in the bathroom and it took a minute to notice Amanda was no longer asleep on the sofa. The sound of running water must mean she was taking a bath or in the shower, he wasn't certain but about then humor kicked in, his mother's old jogging suit was needed and he went in to the utility room to dig it out of a basket load of washed laundry that he had not found time to fold. Opening the door just a smidge, he tossed the suit in and started back to the recliner as the drone of rain hit harder on the windows. He ran out to raise the window to the farm truck and as an afterthought collected the guns. Inside, he turned off the air conditioning unit and raised the front windows to the screened porch.

"No picking, tomorrow, huh? Well, it's a blessing to have made it to the November for this rain, isn't it?" She asked, coming in with a towel wrapped around her hair and wearing the jogging suit. "We're getting a lot of use out of these duds, aren't we? What would your mother think?" Sinking onto the sofa, she said, "I hope I didn't embarrass myself, too much...but I almost know I did something...when I'm tired as I've been lately...I revert to my days of growing up when I would sleep walk and sometimes say things I shouldn't."

"Hmmm. I see. Very intriguing."

"You ask me why wasn't I married?"

"Really? What did you say?"

"That I let the girl of my dreams get away." He went across to sit by her, taking her hand. "Did you ever wonder how our life together could have been and why we've waste so much time we could be together?" When she was quiet, he continued. "I do. The wonder would have been us, you, me and Abby but you didn't want to hear about that life and I told you if you ever did to come to me and we would work it out." He raised her hand to his lips and kissed the finger tips, one by one. "I'm still waiting."

"What about Belinda?"

"I don't know. There's something about her that doesn't fit. I can't put my mind, or should I say heart into it, to ask her to marry me when you are still out there wandering around and every fiber of my being cries out for you, to have you near where I can be with you, protect you..."

"You think I need protecting?"

"It's a figure of speech, but I would if needed." It was at that moment the sound of an explosion and They felt rather than saw something whiz in front of their face. "Get down," was all he had time to say as he was turning out the lights before falling onto the floor beside her.

"The guns are still in the truck," she started to scream but felt his hand over her mouth.

"I brought them in." He half whispered. "Let's stay here, for a minute until we hear a noise or the sound of a vehicle leaving. I don't think anyone will get out with it raining hard and there is lightning."

"But someone shot into the room...if it's true that was a bullet. It could've hit one of us."

"It was a random shot. But you are right, one of us could have been hurt."

"Who would do this?" He was silent. And then she said, "Clark." She felt as though life drained from her body. This was dangerous and she had put Jake in harm's way, not just herself. "This has to stop. I have to talk to him." He could see her face by the light in the hall when she turned to him.

"You can't reason with a mad man, Amanda, and that seems to describe him tonight."

Her voice was half pleading, "he wasn't always like this." He had a firm grip on her hand.

"But he is now, and you can't go to him. He has a gun. He would kill you and not care." Outside lightning flashed earth to sky, and the thunder erupt into a crackling fervor to match. She strained to rise but he wouldn't let her. "No, Amanda. No." He felt her tears on his arm. "Do you care for him that much?"

"No, no. I don't understand it, Jake, but for a while he was not like that."

"Amanda, what if the man had an agenda, you aren't even aware of... for a while there was something challenged him? You can't fall for that. There are decent people...care about them.'

"I do, but he's going to die out there, either the lightning or the Police will take him."

She was beyond upset. He felt her pain and pulled her into his arms. "Amanda. Amanda." He kissed the top of her head, pat her back as one would comforting a child. "Shh. Shh. When we hear the

vehicle move away, we'll get up from here." He was amazed at her grieving cry as he wondered how close to that man, had she been? He couldn't help but ask. "Amanda, do you care for me, at all? Or, is it him?"

"I care for Clark, as one would for a wounded animal, Jake," her whisper was weak and fading, "but Jake, I love you for the man you are, who would care for me in spite of my..." thunder covered her words..." I think I have loved you more each day but I was afraid to say it, to believe there was hope with Belinda in the picture..."

"But you would run out in the rain with bullets flying to save him."

"There have been days I've hated him, Jake, for what he did to me in the world of business. You I have never so much as distrust or...." The thunder and lightning were hitting harder as she talked and curled into the warmth of Jake's body. "I have only grown to love you more each day," she whispered.

He was confused. "The man would hurt you, Amanda. Do not trust him."

"I got the gun, Jake. You know I did, for a reason, for those moments when he is not himself."

"It has been a while," Jake started to rise when gun shots erupted, closer to the house than before. "He's in the back yard." This time he was practically on his stomach heading for the kitchen.

"Don't go out there. Let me. Maybe I can talk him into going back to the clinic." A bullet zipped over them from the back and she heard singing. "He's taunting us." She tried to rise to the side.

"Stay down, Amanda, he will kill you." Jake could smell something burning. "He did this before, what can he be burning, now?" He knew that sound. "Does your car have an alarm? That's it." Jake was scrambling to his feet. "He meant to throw us off, lighting in the front yard but setting fire to your car in the back. But what is that noise I can't identify."

"It's my keys and purse in the car. I didn't lock it because you carried the guns to your truck." Jake was going out the door, thinking to surprise Clark before he pulled the trigger, but Amanda saw him, before he had collected the keys. Too late, she saw Clark swing and Jake went down. It was too dark to see Clark when he moved away. She grabbed one of the guns and ran out into the night. Jake lay on the ground an arm's length from the side of the Jeep. If she could drag him that meager distance, perhaps she could protect them both behind a wheel of the Jeep.

He was dead weight. There was no way she could pull him into the Jeep and the Passenger side had a melted seat where Clark had tried to set it on fire. It was possible it was still burning. Fearing a loose bullet, or worse Clark grabbing hold of her, Amanda dragged Jake around the Jeep and pushed his body in front of the wheel. She tried to think, if Clark thought there was someone else; "Mrs. Turner, come help me," she called out, "Jake needs us; come help me get him on his feet." Farthest from truth, she tried to revive him. "Jake. Jake." She shook him but nothing happened. "Mrs. Turner, come help with your son. He's fallen and he's hurt."

She couldn't see Clark but she felt he stopped moving and listened for someone to come out of the house. All the while she was trying to wake Jake. Just as she heard the sound of Clark running toward the road, Jake began to cough and for the first time she hoped he was all right and would come around. She had bought a little time in trying to make Clark believe Mrs. Turner was in the house.

Right now, she had to get Jake to a doctor, but how was she to move him? Tomorrow would be soon enough to track down Clark. She had a feeling he would not go far. He was out there waiting for her.

Chapter
9

....

"I'm calling for an ambulance," she assured Jake.

"Please, no ambulance. Just let me get my bearings. I think whatever he hit me with was a powerful blow." He was able to place a hand on her arm as she continued to punch in the numbers. "Stop. I can't let them put me in a hospital. I always worry they'll take Abby, thinking I'm a bachelor and not able to see to her needs."

"You don't know that."

His eyes were pleading where his ability to speak at the moment was weak. He pressed on her arm.

Reluctantly, she closed the phone. "Let's get you inside, or into my car, but you'll have to get in the back. I think there's a fire smoldering in the passenger seat."

"Truck?"

She studied the way he looked. If he was coming around, his progress was very slow. "If I can get you into the car, I can take you to Mother's to be with Abby or maybe it would be better to go to my house and not involve them, but," she had a wistful expression, "Clark is fully aware of where I live."

That seemed to bring him to his feet, staggering but on his feet. "Let's go," he said, opening the door to the passenger side, haphazardly slapping the seat to see if it became inflamed and when it didn't, he pulled up the floor mat and pushed it over the seat before he loaded his body into the car.

Shaking her head, she wondered that she had left the keys in the ignition and her purse on the dash. Glancing to be certain the house's splintered door was shut, Amanda backed down the drive, around Jake's truck, and headed toward her house.

They were two miles down the road when they approached a farm truck left stranded across the road. "Careful," Jake, cautioned. "Something doesn't seem right." As weak as he was, he opened the door to get out. "I'll check on it. If anything happens, use the gun."

Amanda watched as he walked around the truck and then came to her side of the Jeep, bending down. "It seems all right. I don't know why it's across the road, but…" At that point, Jake fell back, this time a blow to the back of the head and Amanda found herself being pulled from the Jeep. Clark, took the gun and threw it to one side of the road, and then dragged her some fifty feet to his car. To Amanda it felt like a mile.

"Why are you doing this?"

"Did you really think you could outsmart me? You and lover boy? Well, he ain't so loveable now, is he?" He clicked the fob from his pocket and lights came on from behind a stand of trees. She had driven past them many times and tonight they were just part of the roadside to home. "Get in." He grasp her hand, tighter, making her slide beneath the wheel. Once inside, he dug down into the side panel of the car, brought out a rope and wound it around both of her hands, leaving enough to wrap around the passenger seat. "You comfy, honey," he mimicked as if he was someone who cared. She wasn't. She had seen the brown bottle half wrapped in a brown paper bag. How strong was the stuff he was drinking?

Once his foot hit the gas pedal, they were roaring down the road.

"Please, Clark, this is a country road, you don't know it."

"Who cares? Do you care? Does lover boy care? Does my Momma care?"

"How is your mother?" She tried to sound as though life was normal.

"What do you care? You didn't like her and she didn't like you. Hell, she don't like me." He began to laugh, finally to control the laughter and began to sing in a terrible voice, the same song she had heard before. "When the moon comes up on the mountain, I will dream of you dear…"

She thought, hard, trying to remember the right words. "When the moon comes over the mountain, I'll dream of you, dear." She had barely finished the word. He slapped her hard enough her head flew backwards and she felt the impact as her neck popped.

"You don't sing my song. You hear?" He was screaming at the top of his lungs. "You got it wrong. You hear me?" The car came to a screeching halt, careening one way and then the other as he leaned over her, "If I say sing, you sing and if I don't, you don't sing. You hear me?" With a hand on each side of her head, he made her look at him and then as if the anger dissipated, he calmly turned loose, put the car in gear and began to move forward. Within seconds he was singing his song with its mismatched words, and occasionally sipping from the bottle in the side pocket of the door.

He drove to the next town and the next, sixty miles before coming to the foothills that led to rougher terrain and taking a side road, marked by three mailboxes void of names, turned West into a road overgrown with weeds. The path was barely visible. Wide enough for one vehicle, she wondered what happened if they met another. At the end of the road, she could see buildings. But something was different. Maybe it was the rocks, they were not smooth but jagged, hurtful and scary. The landscape reminded her of a place of hardship, where the rocks would not whisper peace. Fear clutched her heart as tears ran down her cheeks.

"I found our perfect home," he said, his voice exuberant and proud. "You will be my little wifey and I'll be your beau." His eyes were glassy when he turned to her with a smile plastered across his face. "Don't you love that word? Beau. I will be your beau, when the moon comes over the mountain." He sang as he threw an arm around her trying to kiss her on the lips but went amiss, trying then to cover and keep the verse going as he demanded she sing and her eyes watered when he slapped her again, her to quit. "Now we go in and I show you our marvelous honeymoon suite. No crying. No tears."

The door was locked but to her surprise he had a key. Inside, there was a dilapidated sofa, one large chair, a rickety table and a fireplace with age old ashes. Pointing to a faded photo in brown tones on the wall, "Grampa," he said, "an old bastard, if ever there was one. He killed Gramma." She shuddered wondering if he made the story up as they went along or there was truth in the telling. "You can carry in our supplies, after I nap." He wound the rope around her neck and fell onto the sofa, the end of the rope attached to his belt. Forced to bend to his movement, she had to sit in the floor.

Worried, whether Jake had been found, she sit, shoulders hunched forward, her hair hiding her face. "Whack." His hand hitting her full back side brought tears to her eyes. "Sit up straight. Haven't I told you it's important. Do you want to grow up hunch backed?" He slid back into sleep and her shoulders drooped as she managed to turn to be aware when his eyes opened. She was tired enough, had the rope been longer, she would have laid on the floor. By the time he awakened, every bone in her body was aching. "Did I tell you to sit straight?" She did her best. "Sing," he said, "and don't change the words." But he didn't wave his arms and she thought perhaps he was still tired.

She sang throughout the day, mixed with being led to his car to bring in supplies. Strangely, where she envisioned food, there was a bottle of orange juice, two half wrapped hot dogs that looked a few days old and three bottles of whiskey which made her wonder how long the whiskey would last and an unusual jumble of infant toys, old with the rubber cracking, soiled and ready to discard; that box confused her. From time to time, he drank from one of the bottles of whiskey. Her mind lingered on the box of toys and his command for her as though he had been told at one time to sit up straight. Could it be, either his mother or grandmother had been over-bearing or was it the Grampa?

As evening drew to a close and the shadows darkened the room, he sit up as one energized, his movements were quick to make the rope tighten around her neck or force her to hurry in laying back to save more rope burns or the prickly rise of the rope into her skin. Something warned her, a sixth sense perhaps, the time of intense danger was approaching.

"Now we have dinner and then we go to bed." She glanced toward the inner rooms. Her bladder was stretched the limit, but she hoped for privacy when she went and not with a rope tying her to him. As for a bed, she couldn't imagine how it would be if a mattress had been left all these years. Taking stock of a second door beyond the room they were in; she saw a wood kitchen table and a sink with a hand pump. Would he know how to use the pump? She knew because her grandmother kept one when she was small but with the years had let it go. "Did you hear me?" His eyes had taken on that glassy look again. She let her eyes roam the room until she found the bottle, down to maybe a fourth. "I said it's time for dinner and then we go to bed."

"Did your mother say you must wash your hands before you eat?"

"Mummy." He was like a child. "Mummy lived here," he said and sank into silence.

For a spell, he was lost in thought, his fingers placing imaginary words or items on a wall. At first, he was as one soothed but little by little he was losing patience as his face turned red and he screamed in that guttural voice, "Because I said, Mummy's darling only has to do as I say. That's all." Shocked, she tried not to look his way, busying herself with the orange juice, looking for a glass and finding one in the cabinet, filthy with a rim of lipstick dried around the top. As she pushed the handle and waited for a stream of water to come out of the pump, he seemed to evolve from whatever reverie he was in and focus on the glass. Rising fast he caused her to stumble as the rope tightened around her neck and he knocked the glass from her hand. The glass hit the floor and scattered into pieces.

"It's mine. Find your own." Pulling the rope, he reeled her in until they were less than a foot apart.

"Clark," her voice was soft. "Why are you doing this?"

He pushed one of the hot dogs into her hands. "Eat, you can't be sick." When she delayed, he pushed it into her mouth. Rot and mildew covered her lips. He pushed harder against her teeth and she gagged. Not even she meant to spew the vomit onto his shoulders. He slapped her, tightening the rope until she gagged and sank to the floor for mercy. She was tired to the bone and saw no let up as now he seemed either freshly energized or got a kick out of seeing her flail and cry out for help.

When she fell to the floor the second time, a shard of glass was beneath her body. She closed her hand over it, thinking if opportunity struck, she would use it. Blood ran between her fingers and she wiped it aside. Every move he made tightened the rope around her neck. "Get up," he was screaming. "You worthless heap of...." She clasp her hands over her ears; he was looming over her and his arms were raised to hit her.

Without thinking, she kicked out, her feet making contact with his legs, throwing him off balance and down he went, legs wide, arms out without warning to catch himself. He was sputtering and offering cuss words too sensitive to repeat. Amanda was working at the rope, trying desperately to untie it from around her neck where his falling had tightened it to the point it had cut off her air. She grabbed the other end as he dropped it on the floor and scrambled to get up, running for the kitchen, and used the force of her body to open that door. She had no way of knowing there was a steep drop off, just feet from the door and the small deck served no purpose other than to access stone steps that led from the house down to a small lake. She chose the stone steps, falling once feeling the agonizing tear of a jagged edge just below her knee while in her mind she heard her mother saying, run, run, run but the words coming from inside the house were intimidating and in her present state of mind, they were fearful and life threatening. Going farther on the steps, she realized should she fall, she would land in the lake. Running scared, in the dense grass, slipping into the shadows of the trees, when possible, she hoped for a road to find her way out. When she found nothing, she concentrated on sound. For the longest she did not hear him.

She was looking for a place to hide, when all of a sudden, he was right in front of her, his arms open wide to take her to his chest in a strong hold that nearly crushed her body. "Did you really think you could get away from me? You know I have to punish you now." He found the nearest tree of size, placed her against it and begin to wrap the rope around her. "That's not enough, is it?" He, then, slapped her hard enough her head buckled back and then settled on her chest. "That's better. If I say mind, I mean mind." Disgruntled, he began the walk back to the house. He called back. "I'll check with you later."

As glad as she was to see him go, tied fast to the tree, she wondered what would happen to her if he fell asleep. Would he even remember she was with him after drinking all the whiskey in three bottles? If she could rest and gain strength to fight him off, she still had a chance to go home to find Jake. Surely someone had come along the road that led to his house and found him by now, but he had no family to know he was missing. She prayed some of her father's employees would take that road and find him, maybe Dante. Dante seemed to live a life detached and yet willing always to help.

Gnats begin to fly across her face, but there was enough heat of the day there was only an occasional mosquito. That would change as the night come on and darkness settled in. She wasn't sure when she slept but it was completely dark when she awakened and there was no Clark. If she made a guess, it would be that he was comfortably asleep on the bed she had yet to see. She noticed her cheek felt swollen and realized three times he had hit her, with enough force to cause bruises. Her leg felt numb where she had cut it open on the jagged edge of the step but it had bled profusely in the beginning which she supposed cleaned it. The other leg was riddled with mosquito bites she felt, but could do nothing about. She tried to think of Jake. But that only made her worry. Now it was Clark would save her if he remembered he had left her there. She had been foolish to think Clark would change.

Her hopes had been high but Clark would play the same game over and over. What he told her was that his mother was very strict. He wasn't certain she loved him because he seemed never to please her. His posture and his speech were not pleasing to his mother. Clark remembered the wrong things. He had been almost childlike when they visited friends with a small puppy. At first, he seemed loving with it and then about thirty minutes into the visit he became angry, doubled a fist and hit the little dog and stirred up the couple's child. He finally cooled down enough to apologize and whisk her out the door and to his mother's home. Now, she wondered was that why someone as talented as Clark, whose name was well known, ended up working in the next town. Had his temper flared and he had attacked the wrong person?

What was the underlying cause of his rage that he had to control a person? She considered other people's way of handling life. Not everyone got by with hitting another person or destroying who they were. She drift off to sleep to awaken in the dark of night, rain pelting her arms where she had folded them in front of her body. There was no moon. She had sunk down onto the ropes but still they would not loosen. The rain increased and all she could do was let her head fall to her chest and pray he would remember he left her there in the forest.

She knew she was dehydrated. Her belly rumbled for lack of food. She had been tied to the tree probably fifteen hours by now. When the rain began, she lift her head and let it run into her mouth. If God was seeing to that need, perhaps he had other plans in motion for her to be found. Clark would still be asleep and she was unsure of Jake, but one thing she knew he was aware she was gone and already if able, Jake was trying to find her. It was a new day.

By mid-evening, she had been tied to the tree a full twenty-four hours. She doubt the mosquitoes could find a spot on her body to bite. Her physical body was taking a beating and her mind was slowing down. She couldn't give up. No one died from loss of food, did they? In today's world? As dark closed in her head had not raised the last hour, all the thoughts concerning Clark had not produced an answer. The only thing she surmised was the coldness of his mother with one weak moment in that staunch façade, called Mrs. Benson. "He had a brother, a genius, kind and gentle, but he died and Clark is what we have left." Perhaps, Clark's mother's reserved but haughty way made her want to help him.

Hanging helpless on the ropes tied to the tree, Amanda slipped into a world of sleeping, half aware that she was in the forest, fully aware she needed help and her dreams filled with Jake and Abby. She knew time by the cracked face of her watch. At times, her parents drift through, always carrying Abby, letting her down, back up, safe in their arms. "Jake. Jake." She whispered from the depth of sleep, "I'm asking Jake. Do you still want me?"

Miles from Jericho, James Ferguson, paused again to wonder why he was having strange dreams. Tonight, as the rain continued, he checked the supply room to see that all was in order and then spoke with the night person before he retired to his home in back of the motel. What was her name, the one who helped with lifting Lois back onto the bed?

It was nights like this he missed his wife most. He would watch the news at eight o'clock and then go to bed. Right now, he settled into his old recliner and listened to the locals on a program that discussed the latest happenings in and around town. Their talk became such a lull he found himself sinking into a sleep that was restful until he began to have one dream over and over. He was having lunch with that girl that came through last year right after Christmas, what was her name? Half asleep, he heard, "and now it's time for news around the world in five minutes."

He must have really dropped off, he thought the news man mentioned a woman missing from, was that…did he say Jericho? Man, some one must have dropped something in his coffee. But she was a nice girl, seemed down on her luck, maybe like if a man had treated her wrong and her Christmas, like his, was ruined.

⟨∞⟩

"Jake?" Phyllis called but he didn't hear. He was sitting in the chair opposite Charles in his wheelchair. He had been there overnight, afraid if Amanda called, he wouldn't be there to hear her voice. "Charles, are you watching the television?"

"No, Phyllis, I'm like Jake. I'm sitting here waiting for our girl to call, but I'm not dead on my feet as he is for lack of sleep. We've got to get him into a shower and in a bed to rest tonight. He won't be any good to himself or her if someone calls and says they've found her."

"Right now, I want you both to come to the table. I've made a pot of stew and it's got good vegetables to work with our situation right now." She turned to check on Abby before going to the kitchen. "This one's all right. Now, Charles, see if you can get Jake to the table."

Charles wheeled over to Jake and laid a hand on his knee. "Son, wake up. I want you to wash up and let's get to the table so we can pray for Amanda."

"Yes, Sir. I will." He was so far gone, Charles thought of how a robot would sound but he knew Jake cared. When he'd come to the house two nights past to see if Amanda made it home, he was sick of everything that had a hand in their daughter's being missing. He had tried every avenue in his book and Charles but there was not a trace of Amanda. He thought she was with Clark Benson and if that was the man he'd seen, something was wrong with him. And then that strange text had come through and he had deleted it. Only someone crazy would send that text. The police had a different opinion. Charles and Phyllis filed a missing person report and ran a front-page ad in the newspaper. No one had heard anything.

Their appetites were lacking. Finally, Phyllis collected the dishes and cleared the table. Pouring fresh coffee into the cups she sit down at the table to try to talk the two men out of the depressive state they seemed to be slipping into.

"Guys, we have to keep the faith, if not for ourselves, for Amanda. If, it is as you think, Jake, that something was more wrong with that fellow, then we are going to have to buckle down and pray specifically. Our prayers for Amanda may be all she has right now, if she is lost or if things are better than we think, but in case they are worse, lets talk to the Lord." She waited, watching them bow their head.

"Father, Lord, thank you that you are Lord of our lives. We give you praise and honor as we come to you. Our hearts are heavy. We don't know if Amanda is alive, or somewhere in danger, hurt or in dire need of help but we feel it is serious, extremely serious, Lord, or she would have called us, and that is why we come to you, right now, asking you to give her strength to handle whatever she is facing. We ask you to touch her body that harm does not come to her body, to touch her mind that she does not despair or give up, that she clings to you Lord that no matter what happens or has happened or will that you are with her sustaining her and Lord that not another day goes by without the one we love receiving help that comes from you when all else fails. We don't know where she is, Lord, but you do. We know she is in your hands. We know Lord you can use someone else to find her and we pray for that person. Help us to do what we are supposed to and bless those trying to help us. Thank you, Father. Amen"

"Thank you, Phyllis," Jake said. "I pray but it wouldn't make sense to anyone else."

Thirty six hours had passed since Clark tied her to the tree. Rain continued through the night and left behind unseasonal cold weather. While many voiced concerns for cotton in the field, as many considered the where-about of Amanda Lanis. It was rumored she had been kidnapped. No one had information whether she knew the kidnapper or not. "She was abducted on her way home," her employees were told and they elected to scout the area to see if she had been left behind if it was true the abductor fled.

⟡

Woodsey and Dante' chose to step into Amanda's office for a private discussion.

"This is something," Dante began. "I don't know what to say to the men when they ask questions.

"You've been doing fine," Woodsey replied. "It's none of their business who she knew, but it is their business to know she was taken by someone and no one has an idea where she was taken. That's what concerns me most of all."

"They want to broaden the search but that would be a wild goose chase." Frustration was in Dante's voice and shone on his face. "You would think someone had a clue. Even the Police say they don't."

"It's not like Amanda, so that lets me know she didn't go by choice." Woodsey was interrupted by the ringing of his cell. "You mind if I get this?" Dante nodded. "Hello," Woodsey said and after that he listened, putting the phone on speaker.

"I spoke with you, weeks past, concerning Clark Benson. I told you the family hires me to keep tabs on him. I can tell you he is nowhere near Crimson Springs, nor Calder Mountain, where his phone signal is coming through. His phone has possibly been stolen. However, I heard on the news you have a lady from your community that is missing. It would be wise to check the area where that signal is coming from. She may have his phone in her possession. That's all. Do not try to contact me."

Woodsey had to get his bearings; his mind was on a rush, trying to remember the voice he'd heard when he was alone. The voice he'd told Amanda had brought warning for her to be careful. He couldn't read anymore in to this message than that one, but it appeared that the person that he hadn't seen, was very much real. Blood rushed to his face, "I've got to go see the Police," he said. "Come drive me, I'll explain on the way. I can't drive. I'm too excited. Maybe this is it."

The Police were not into believing Woodsey at first. "Call Amanda's daddy," he said. "He'll tell you."

"Who is this woman's daddy?" Their expressions changed when Woodsey said, "Charles Lanis."

"That's the woman we're looking for, already," the captain exclaimed. "Why didn't you say so? Her daddy called and ask us if we had seen that fellow we picked up before, and Charles said his daughter hadn't come home."

"Excuse me, I told you, Amanda Lanis." Woodsey was giving Dante the look. "Let's go."

The two walked out. "We better put gas in the truck," Dante said. At that moment, Jake and Amanda's daddy pulled in. They met them at the curb. "No need getting out, they're spinning their wheels. We are gassin' up, ready to move within thirty minutes. Charles, you need to stay here and man the phones, but Jake needs someone riding with him. That way we got another set of eyes and ears when we get there."

"I got just the person," Charles said. "Our new pastor. He is a woodsman, I hear, and could be handy." He was already going through his phone directory. "Jake, if you will drop me off at Phyllis, I think Amanda would be glad to know we are together and I'll get to hold that sweet baby a bit more."

"Charles," Jake was about to caution.

Charles waved a hand in dismissal, "I know. I know, don't jump the gun, right, but I got this feeling."

Woodsey and Dante ran Charles back to Phyllis house, returning to join Jake and the new Pastor to find Amanda .

"I am assuming the young lady in question, is in some sort of house, correct?" The new pastor had come on board, pleasant and wanting to use the drive to Calder Mountain, to learn as much as needed.

"We don't know. In fact, the trip to the foothills to the mountains is barely noticeable. Funny thing, though, I've never been to Calder Mountain and it's within seventy miles from Jericho. I find stories about it interesting."

"Such as?" Pastor asked, "Because I had never visited Jericho before and when we were called to pastor, I was very interested." For a second he glanced up to the sky. "Listen to that rain but go on."

"Well, you know how our rocks around home are for the most part smooth? Calder has sharp edged rocks; we are told are hard on a person should they fall." He glanced pastor's way, "but that's beside the point, isn't it? If that fellow is as wealthy as I've heard, the rocks don't matter, soft or hard. Right?" Jake began to go over the evening, hour by hour, and then he spoke.

"I don't know what could have gone wrong? Abby was with Amanda's mother and I was driving Amanda back to her house." For a mile, Jake drove as the evening began to lose its hours and to the Pastor, Jake seemed lost in thought and he waited for him to continue the story. "One minute we were riding along, the next stopped by a stranded vehicle that was horizontal across the road." He shook his head to stop thinking past the moment. "In your opinion, what do we do first?"

"Once we arrive, we will assess the situation and then we'll know what's most necessary."

They made the sixty miles from Jericho. Jake drove slower once inside the forest looking for a spot recently inhabited. When they found one of possibility, with four trees stripped of bark and shining in the rain, they stopped and opened the first cannister of items they might need. "First, fellows," Pastor said, "We hold hands and we pray. We can do nothing on our own but with God, anything is possible and that's who we want on our side." He prayed and then he gave each man a small round object about two inches long. "These are whistles, of a gentle nature. Once we get in the woods, we will start with Jake, then Woodsey, Dante and me. They tell us where each other walks. They are low key whistles, I've seen them used effectively, in dire situations." With the rain pelting their faces, he said, "Looks like this is one." He finished, "We must stay in touch. We cannot add anyone to the mystery. We start together and come back out together."

They were in the forest an hour without finding anything pertaining to the situation. Pastor blew the whistle for them to regroup and discuss the matter. "What are you receiving?" Pastor asked Jake. "I 've been watching you since we all returned and something is weighing on your mind. I know it happens so just tell us what you're thinking."

"I feel a bit confused by the whole thing, but it is implanted in my head that there's a house nearby."

"Nothing shows on the map," Dante said, "But I'm willing to look for one, maybe the person who took Amanda would be there." His words dropped low as Jake's cell rang and Dante gave him time to answer.

"Yes, Sir, how did you get my name and number? I don't believe we've met." Jake put his cell on speaker. "Mr. Ferguson, yes, yes, sir."

"Mr. Jake Turner?" Mr. Ferguson was a calm man, seldom upset since losing his wife; her illness and losing her was the hard part. "I was listening to the news and it said if you have any news concerning Amanda Lanis of Jericho…" You might think this silly my calling and the Lord knows I've thought it over…but the last few days and just now as I was watching television, I keep seeing Amanda and my eyes are wide open and I think its her. Can I talk with her?"

"Uh," Jake cleared his throat, "Mr. Ferguson, you may not be aware of this but the girl you thought so much of," He struggled, "you may not know our Amanda has been taken and we are right now in the process of hunting for her. I don't mean to cut you short but could we talk maybe….later?"

Ferguson's voice became stronger. "No, Son, we need to talk now. Don't hang up. It's about your wife. Here's something I don't understand either but I don't think I'm bad news by calling you about her if you want to know where she is." Silence met silence now. And suddenly Jake was listening hard.

"Aamanda made quite an impression on me, so just know as I'm by myself all the time and I turn on television for company I heard this little bit of news, an Amanda of Jericho has been missing and I think to myself, is this real? I never did this before but I've been seeing a dream about Amanda Lanis and I go back to the office and look back on the books to be sure that's her last name and there it is, Amanda Lanis, or was, so I hurried back to call you."

"Mr. Ferguson what did you dream?"

"Well, I'm not sure exactly it's a dream, its so real and most times I have my eyes wide open, but it's like she went to this old house and there's a problem, I can't tell if she's hurt or her feelings are badly hurt…but something's wrong. Anyway, this old house is almost in the woods and there's just one road in and the house has been let go for years so I don't know why she's there. I don't hear well, so I can't understand if the name of the town is Cold or not and there's a mountain, so the television just now said any news on Amanda Lanis of Jericho and showed a number to call, that's when I got you."

"Mr. Ferguson," Jake's voice held excitement. "I will call you back and thank you for calling." He turned to the others waiting and wondering why he got excited all of a sudden. "Fellows, maybe we are in the right area with a lot of trees in between. We have got to find a road that is hardly visible, maybe never used and a house at the end of that road. Let's get our stuff together." It wasn't until he and the pastor were in the truck looking for a barely visible road along the way that he realized he had a minister of the Bible teaching, but more important a minister of God with him, and it dawned on him many did not believe in what they were involved in at the moment. "Pastor," he said, "I apologize if you aren't a believer that God works in mysterious ways but if we find Amanda, that's what this is, Him working in mysterious ways."

Pastor didn't reply but when they heard the whistle, "Praise the Lord," he said. "We needed this right now." Jake was kicking himself, "I drove right by it, wouldn't you know." But no one cared because they all were laughing, but, "now," said Pastor, "to find the house and find what we are looking for."

Dante spotted the house, which brought cheers from all of them. Once they had seen the inside, the joy was misplaced and they were seriously dreading how they would find her but not one uttered the worst fear of all.

Woodsey discovered the blood on the jagged edged step and it increased his worry. "She's hurt and has been in a down pour of rain since yesterday and it was cool last night in the woods if we find her there. My guess is he broke her spirit the day before with ridicule and meanness," Woodsey picked up his work bag and started down the stairs, they didn't need to see his emotions.

Dante hurried to catch Woodsey. "What are you thinking? It did turn colder last night and out in this weather, she is hurt, isn't she, or she would have made it back to the house?" Woodsey was so quiet, he reached out to grab his arm. "It can't be that, Woodsey. She was a good person; nobody has the right to take another's…"

Woodsey cut him off, "Don't say it. Not one of us wants to hear that."

They heard one of the whistles and walked horizontally, hoping as planned they'd meet somewhere in the middle rather than to keep going forward. "What now?" It was plain his worrying was taking a toll on him. "It did stand to reason, the man would go a straight path from the house, doesn't it? I doubt he knew where he was and just followed the way back…I mean if he was drinking heavy."

"We saw those bottles. Empty bottles," Dante nodded. "Three, wasn't it?

"What do you say, Pastor?" Jake backed up against a tree. "I'm doubting the guy that called and yet, I believe he had most of it right."

"Let's each say how we expected to find her, maybe our method is what's wrong. I was afraid she would be laying on the ground, unable to move but shaking from the cold."

"Similar," Woodsey agreed, "but hurt bad."

Dante agreed, "but I thought as tough as she is, she would be locked onto an object. You know hanging on."

"Jake?" they all waited, hoping there was a light on what they'd missed.

"Listening to you all, I think we've all tried to think it through but we can't because we don't know. Now, I wonder if we've missed it, and it scares me nearly to death, what if he hung her in a tree?"

"He's a rich boy that's used to things handed to him, he won't have energy to do that, Jake, but what if she's not laying on the ground because it's been cold and instead, she's been tied to the tree, and maybe can't get loose. If we don't look closely, we won't see that. Let's try a different method, and let's be positive we're going to find her." Dante started walking back the direction he and Woodsey came from. "I'm going to say, a path from the house is more likely." Dante for some reason kept his eyes on Pastor.

"Fellows, I believe we need to take a moment with the Lord. Let's do this silently, from our heart. Let's thank the Lord that Jake got the call and let's believe it was meant for us to give us something positive, as Dante said, and then we'll continue on. When you finish, just move on down the trail."

She must have awakened, not remembering the last time she'd fallen asleep, her weight was fell onto the ropes, regardless of the prickly nature of the rope cutting into her skin. She managed to glance down at her feet, swollen out of the shoes she was wearing. It was her leg where the stone ledge cut and made it bleed that worried her. There had been a lot of bleeding. Her shoe was full of it. Maybe it wasn't as bad as it looked, but if it was, without antibiotic an infection could develop and no better than she could see, that leg looked larger than the other.

Miserable, soaking wet, there was no doubt Clark had forgotten her and he would never remember. She raised her head, the phlegm nearly choking her, her nose was stuffy, and her head ached. No doubt she'd have pneumonia from this mess. She coughed and then the coughing wouldn't stop. She coughed until her dry throat produced blood in the phlegm. Exhausted, she tried not to sleep, but her body had lost all defense, first she felt her lashes touch her cheek and fought to open her eyes, her head slumped against her chest and while she realized she was not with Jake, she saw him dancing Abby around the room, Abby squealing and loving every minute of it. Slipping into a sleep of no return, she whispered, "Will you still want me."

Jake stopped abruptly. "Do you hear that?" Pastor gave him a critical glance before he looked the direction Jake was pointing. He shook his head. "It sounded like someone coughing, a woman. She would be coughing by now, out in the rain all this time." He turned toward where he'd heard the sound. "I know I heard something." He began to run, stopping ever so many feet to listen, but there was no sound. Pastor followed and at the first stop, blew into his whistle. In minutes Woodsey and Dante were standing by his side. Pastor pointed to Jake, running ahead.

"Did she call?" Woodsey had been thinking they'd start hearing something soon. He was wet, what wasn't rain was sweat. "She didn't call out?" He couldn't understand why Pastor was hanging back. "Either she did or didn't."

"She didn't," Pastor said. "He thinks he heard a woman coughing." At that moment, a sound reached their ears.

"That ain't coughing, that's someone strangling," Woodsey exclaimed. "Someone that's been out in the rain too long." He began to run after Jake. "I believe our boy's found our Mandy." Now they all followed the direction Jake was going. In the shadows of the forest, they couldn't see far ahead, but when they round a stand of trees there was Jake, his arms around a tree; but when they moved closer, they saw Amanda folded up, more than standing, tied to the tree, her hair wet and molded to her forehead, while she was completely lifeless with no need for the supplies they'd brought. It appeared she was dead. They were devastated but Jake wasn't giving up.

"She looks feverish," Woodsey said and Dante nodded.

"Amanda, Amanda." Jake looked to the Pastor. "Didn't I see a stethoscope in your supplies. Please, listen to her heart." Jake had all but the last knot untied of the rope, one more and he could take her into his arms.

Pastor was removing the pack from his back, while Dante and Woodsey's expression of pity and pain were so evident, he already knew their disappointment. He intended to hand the instrument to Jake, but Jake declined, saying, "Please, Pastor, listen to her heart." Pastor listened, his own countenance sad, again he pressed the instrument into the lower area of Amanda's heart and listened again. "I guess we want it so bad; it almost seems I pick up a faint beat, but then it's gone. Here, Dante." He beckoned Dante closer and helped hook the stethoscope in his ears.

Dante listened, his sad face deepening and then, it was as if he straightened suddenly as he said, "I believe it's there, her heart is so faint, it's struggling because it's so tired, right, Pastor?" He turned to Pastor and grabbed him, with Woodsey next, but he had a question. "What do we do now, we can't lose the heart beat in moving her and she is burning up."

Pastor was finding the fever thermometer and wondering if in her state he should try to use it. "We can't do anything, anyway, let's forego this one," he said. "Do you suppose we could get Jake's truck this far into the forest?" For a minute, their faces were a study, contemplating the terrain they'd walked and the huge slabs of jagged rock sticking out of the ground that they had avoided. Pastor knew these were the men that cared and would do nothing to jeopardize Amanda.

Woodsey spoke, "We can if we walk ahead and alongside to be careful that we don't puncture a tire and get stranded." He placed a hand on Jake's shoulder, "You okay with our plan?" Jake nodded. "Then the three of us are going for the truck, yours, do you have the keys? And it might bring comfort if we call Mr. Charles and Miss Phyllis."

Jake gave him the keys, and whispered, "thank you." He was almost in tears. "She doesn't even hear me, Woodsey."

"That's why we are going to get her out of here, pronto. A few days treatment and she will."

It was a tedious task, with many side-moves of seeking a new path when an immovable object appeared that they were not equipped to navigate, but by five o'clock they had severed their association with Calder Forest and had no reason to return to the house, but they did wonder that Clark Benson had seemed familiar with the property.

The y traveled as before, the Pastor and Jake together with Jake sitting in the back holding Amanda.

They were in the last thirty miles back when they met the Jericho Police. Pastor was driving with the emergency lights flashing and when the head car saw he would not stop, that car turned and led the way to Jericho's hospital.

Only then did Pastor chuckle, "They must have run the plates," he said. "I'll have to say there must have been a lot of red tape to just now believe what Woodsey told them and be on the way to try to find the location." He glanced back at Jake's grim face. "Still no response?" Jake shook his head. "We are almost there, just hang on, God is with us."

The Police must have alerted the hospital. As they drove in, medical people rushed through the doors with a gurney. Within minutes, Amanda was in the throes of several doctors and nurses and the four were sitting in the waiting room.

"Excuse me," Pastor said. "I need to call Charles and Phyllis and tell them we're here with their daughter." It was not by accident Charles had called his doctor and ask him to be the one to be in charge of Amanda's hospital stay.

⁂

It was midnight when the doctor came out to speak with the four and a few members from church who had come to pray for Amanda. Jake stepped forward. "Are you the…" he began, but Jake said, "What can you tell us?" Pastor, Dante and Woodsey stood behind Jake and Phyllis and Charles were within hearing distance, sitting to one side with sleeping baby, Abby. The doctor saw Charles nod his head and began.

"Of course, Miss Lanis suffered from severe hypothermia when you brought her in, understandable if she was out in the rain the last two days and with the weather change. Her heart worked hard during those times, which explains you thought it unusually faint, and that we don't know about as we have no records. The cut on her leg bled enough to cleanse it, but there still remains the danger of an infection setting up, judging by the evidence of enormous swelling. We, as I said, do not have previous records, and we rely on the form her mother submitted. It seems after age twelve she simply did not see a doctor."

"What about the cough?" Jake corrected, "She didn't cough on the ride here, but that's how we found her, she was coughing, and then a strangling sound and I wonder why she hasn't coughed since…and does she have Pneumonia?"

"She does have other symptoms and we have put her on antibiotics, for the Pneumonia and the danger of infection to the leg."

"Can I see her?" Once more, unknown to Jake, the doctor glanced to Charles and Charles nodded.

⁂

They bathed Amanda and had her on i.v.'s. She was covered from the neck down in a number of blankets and still her body was shaking but her eyes were closed as if in sleep. A nurse entered without his knowing and seeing the expression on his face, she began to explain. "We feel she is cold throughout and that's the reason for that many blankets. She is dehydrated, thus the I.v.'s. Her color may seem a bit ruddy because she is still running temperature but it is dropping and the rise there below the knee is for the bandage around her leg where the deep gash occurred." Not knowing if he registered a word she had said, or if he did whether there was any comfort, the nurse sought to take his mind from the obvious thought that she was dying. "She's a beautiful young woman, we did the best we could with her hair, and I'd say when you return in the morning, you will see a difference in your wife."

"She's not my wife. I ask her…but…no….we….. not yet."

He heard the nurse say, "I'll give you a minute alone with her." He had held the fear as long as he could. He had to turn loose. Wasn't that what Pastor told him? "Turn loose and trust." He practically fell onto the bed, his hand on hers. "Wake up, Amanda, wake up." It finally hit him; she had parents outside of the room that wanted to see their daughter. There were no words to express what he was feeling.

The next week was draining. He asked Phyllis if she mind keeping Abby longer each day. "No, dear," she replied, "she feels like our own, now and she is a good child." He spent most of his time at the hospital, praying Amanda awakened. There had been a day when they thought Amanda's kidneys were shutting down, all part of the standing outside in the rain those long hours. Just being there, made him feel better. Next week, if it didn't rain, he would be back in the fields; he had to get the crop in, but the time would come too soon to leave her again.

Chapter

10

....

T he ground had dried enough after the rains to finish harvest. Two weeks into November, Jake couldn't believe how time had passed, and if it wasn't for the rain, they would have finished. He returned to his men and the cottonfield, and he wondered that Charles seemed to be a bit standoffish. He had noticed it the last visits he made to see Amanda when he ran into Charles and Phyllis visiting their daughter. Of course, those times, Phyllis would have Abby in her stroller, usually asleep.

"I guess your men are going strong?" He asked before leaving.

"Seems they are," Charles replied and that was the essence of their conversation. He wondered about Amanda's absence from the office and ask, "How are you making it at the office without Amanda?"

Charles seemed reluctant to reply. Jake glanced at Phyllis. When their eyes met, he knew she wanted to say something and it bothered him that she didn't. He turned to leave and was half way down the hall when someone touched his arm.

"Jake?" Phyllis said, "Let's step around the corner, if you got a minute." He followed her. "Jake, I know you are wondering about Charles, aren't you?" Jake nodded. "Just put any worry out of your mind. Charles is blaming himself for asking Amanda to come home." She sighed. "I told him as long as she associated with Clark Benson there was bound to be a problem. He's just let himself get tied up in a knot." And then she almost laughed. "Not to mention he's working again, not sitting watching Dana White on television."

"What are they saying about Amanda, anything new? Something seemed different, to me."

"She's been running temperature, again and they're thinking it has to do with that ugly gash on her leg. There are several different problems and they're meeting to decide what to do."

"Do you mind letting me know? Phyllis, why doesn't she wake up?"

With sad eyes, Phyllis replied, "they say her body suffered such trauma it's resting and what the body accepts, the mind perceives. The mind has to catch up. If that makes any sense." She assured him she would stay in touch. "It's not like we don't see each other every day." She watched him walk on down the hall. He seemed so alone, even with Abby. Again, she realized what her daughter was missing.

Fair Acres finished harvest first. Jake's crew finished the day before Thanksgiving. Jake celebrated, going to see Amanda that evening before picking up Abby from Phyllis. It was heart breaking she looked the picture of health, but something still wasn't one hundred percent right. He had noticed a flurry of activity as he went upstairs and found it was inside Amanda's room.

One of the nurses had become friendly with Jake and whispered to him, "Don't panic, it will be all right. Amanda is in a medically induced coma." He followed her, practically breathing his why question into her ear. "They do this to alleviate pain to the patient." Jake wasn't sure what right he had to question, but he couldn't turn loose of Amanda at this point. That night he was practically glum when he picked up Abby from Phyllis house. He didn't realize until they reached home and he was putting Abby to bed that Charles was still there and what's more he was wearing pajamas and sitting watching the evening news in a new recliner.

"Lord, help me," he slapped his forehead. "The man's sick and I didn't pay any attention." His second thought was to wonder about the new chair. "Like if I deserve knowing anything." For the first time in a while, he smiled, picking up Abby and dancing around, "Wouldn't your Amanda get a kick out of seeing her momma and daddy spending the night together?" Abby, cutting a new tooth, grinned and the slobber dripped onto his face. "That's the only sugar I ever get," he said, lowering her from up in the air to his shoulder. "You are gonna be one toothy ill girl."

After putting Abby to bed, he returned to the piano and sit playing songs he and Amanda had played together. For some reason he branched off into one he had written but never put music to. As he worked, he began to feel the tension leave his body. It was as if God was saying, you say you trust me, you say you believe I can work miracles, but you worry to the point it's making an old man out of you. Why don't you lighten up, you do your work and I'll do mine."

Words began to flow and when the clock struck ten, exhausted, physically and emotionally spent, he lay the pen aside, closed the piano and went to bed. "Lord," he prayed. "I can give her up, if that's your will, but it will be painful." His prayers were intent, asking healing for Amanda. "I love her Lord, but if she needs someone else, then I will try to be happy in your will for her."

Amanda felt the stirrings of her body. Her legs tried to move but her feet felt as though she wore socks. Laced up socks? What? Her door to the room was open. She didn't move her feet when anyone came in. The bed sheets were another story, while she reveled in their fresh smell, the hem of the sheet loved being creased over and over between her fingers. Was she alive? Surely, she was, or else everyone looked so earthly in heaven. She would know the truth if Jake came to see her.

Mid-evening the hospital brought the board of directors through, to see the effectiveness of the remodel. Amanda didn't want to hear the questions and came across as being asleep. They weren't in the room long when she heard one say to another. "This is the room of the woman who was abducted. As I recall you once dated the man that visits here often."

"Oh, my goodness, Shelly, they didn't make you administrator of the hospital for nothing, did they? Did you not know Jake and I are getting married? He is trying to let her down easy. Poor thing."

"No, I'm sorry, I didn't know. What about the little girl? Will you keep her?"

"That will take some time, I'm afraid. Jake has gotten quite attached to her. She's cute, but I don't plan to have children. Our life will be too busy with his farming and our travels."

"Well, the others went on to the room we use for therapy, I thought you might like to check how this one is doing. They brought her out of the medically induced coma yesterday."

"No, we could have skipped her. I'm here to keep my name on the Board of Directors."

Amanda couldn't have hurt more if someone had hit her with a bat to the back of the head. All the times she thought Jake cared, but then, she had not been focusing too well of late and she had no idea how many days. There were times she thought she heard his voice but that must have been a dream.

Jake didn't come to visit that night and she was glad. The next morning when the doctor made his rounds, he discovered Amanda had awakened from what they all considered a bad dream.

He checked her vitals. "How are you feeling?"

"I want to go home." He chuckled. "I'm serious. I can go to my parents if there's a question."

"Not this soon, Miss Lanis. It's for your own good."

"I'm leaving in an hour," she said. "It would be nice if you dismissed me."

She would have been wrong if she thought any other way, a decision to dismiss her meant they would insist only if there was someone to stay with her. In view of why she was in the hospital in the first place, with her abductor still out there, it was wise she stay with someone.

"You want to be dismissed? Why?" Charles Lanis studied his daughter. "What are you not telling us?"

"Nothing, Dad. Is it a problem if I stay with one of you? I thought Mom would let me."

"Hon, either one of us wants you, except it's not just one of us, things have changed."

Her hopes fell. "I can go to my house. I'm sure I'll be okay."

"No, Babe," he fell into her childhood name. "It's not that. Your Mom and I are back together. When we thought we'd lost you we were so upset we found we missed each other and we need each other, so when you are well, we will remarry. We want you."

"Dad, I don't think I can go back to the farm for a while."

"That's all right, Babe. First things first. After you are well, you can decide what you want to do."

"And Dad, when Jake comes to visit, I don't want to be around. Can you live with that, you and Mom?"

"Do you want to talk about it?"

"No, I can't. And I hope you won't talk about it either. Maybe in time, but not now."

Jake returned to the hospital to see Amanda the day after she was dismissed. No one knew where she was going. After work, he arrived at Phyllis to pick up Abby. Phyllis hollered, "Come in. We're in the kitchen. He found Abby pulled up to one of the straight back chairs, patting the seat and jabbering. "That's new," Phyllis explained. "I think she finds the chair her friend. She likes being on her feet."

"So that's what she wants to do?" He picked up his little girl and gave her a kiss. "I missed you."

"Da-da," Abby said, patting his cheeks before she tried to bite his nose.

"Ow, Abby." He waited until Phyllis turned to see what Abby had done. "Phyllis, where's Amanda?" She seemed hesitant to look to where he was standing and when she did, they stared at each other.

"Jake, is there a problem between you two? I can only tell you that Amanda is in a safe place to heal."

"Is she healing from what that monster did to her, Phyllis? Because I'm in the dark."

"She wouldn't tell us. She won't stay in touch with us if we say more. But I can tell you this. She's sad, I worry over her coming out of whatever has hurt her, and I'm talking about more than Clark Benson."

"But I love her, Phyllis."

"I believe you do, Jake, and I think she loves you, but you are going to have to trust in the Lord and bide your time just like Charles and I. I'm very concerned, Jake, and if you value us as friends, then help us to protect her and abide by her wishes until her body heals."

Jake shuddered, "Did he physically molest her, Phyllis? Is that what this is about? I'll kill him."

"I don't know." Phyllis wiped a tear from her cheek with the hem of her apron. "I don't know." She turned back to the stove so he couldn't see her face. "This is very hard, Jake. I can't ask you to dinner Thanksgiving, in case Amanda will have dinner with us. I want to so badly, but she won't come, if…"

"That's fine, Phyllis. It would have been wonderful, all of us together, but I do…I'll help protect her."

∽❧∾

When Jake brought Abby to Phyllis, Amanda was out of sight, but when he left Amanda greeted Abby and Abby's squeals of delight warmed all their hearts. "Momma," Abby said, and Phyllis and Amanda wondered where she had heard the name. "I think it, possibly, is you calling me, Mom," Phyllis said. If Abby loved Jake, it was equally obvious she loved Amanda and Amanda loved her.

"I did not have loving this baby in my plans," Amanda said, one day, "but I have no choice in the matter. My heart belongs to her and I cannot do otherwise." Wisely, Phyllis remained silent.

Thanksgiving arrived. They were in their family home. Phyllis cooked the traditional meal and sent a plate to Dante and Jake. The day went out as quietly as it dawned. Amanda spent the day in her room.

"Mom, I think I'd like to go home. Would that bother you?"

"Are you strong enough? What about when Abby comes? She will miss you."

"I know. I'll come by to see her. I want to make peace with Christmas, Mom. While I was gone, there were no joyous ones. I missed you and Dad and was too proud to come home, it wasn't home anymore. You were one place and he was another. I missed the decorating, the baking, all of it, but I suffered in silence and let the hardness settle around my heart."

"What about now? Are you letting that same hardness destroy what is given to us as a gift, larger than anything we can imagine, that little baby born in a manger while angels sang Christ was born?"

"I remember grandmother had decorations and I have a feeling they are right where she left them."

"You plan to put up a tree and everything?"

"That remains to be seen, as you say, everything…but some of it. Will you drive me. My car's there."

It was a cool day when Phyllis drove her home. Jake had paperwork to do at home and was keeping Abby. "I'll come in and see if everything is all right."

"You don't have to hover over me Mom. My body is weak, but I think my brain functions okay."

"I want to help you carry in the decorations; the doctor said you are not to strain lifting."

"Really? I don't think I could, anyway." Amanda seemed to store that piece of information. "I think I know where she kept decorations, come with me and we will bring them in." Together they dragged the container full of Christmas items into the kitchen. "While I inventory, mom, play the piano."

Phyllis sits at the piano, while Amanda brought items from the large container. Silent Night seemed appropriate as she watched her daughter, and she wondered how would Jake take being turned away, for she knew Amanda would be true to her word and not see Jake and she could only wonder the reason.

Settling into each day was not as easy as she thought it would be, having worked previously, now there were hours to fill and even handicapped by weakness at times, she found herself walking to the window, wondering what life had next in store for her. The Police called often. There was no word as to Clark Benson being found. It was their opinion, either his family was hiding him or he was in a facility learning how to deal with his problem. "We try to drive by to see if everything looks normal," they said. The locks had been changed and an alarm system added. She wished neither was needed.

Charles and Phyllis were waiting Amanda's return to church. "Jake isn't there," her father said, "If that's what's keeping you from attending." She didn't ask why Jake left. Deacon Baumgarten was still there, it seemed and she wondered what he could think knowing she was abducted. Nothing mattered.

The house was decorated. It was an unusually warm day for December and she was restless. There was a strand of lights she tried to hang on the house but had become aware she wasn't steady on the ladder and maybe should wait until Dante was free to help her, but she would have to call him. She had to do something. Through the window she saw the lawn, ankle deep in leaves. "A fire hazard," she muttered. That settled it, changing into denims, tying her hair back, she found a rack and a barrel to empty buckets of leaves in to, and as the evening past she found she enjoyed the task. Pile after pile went into the large bucket to be emptied into the barrel and as the sun was setting, she was standing staring at the barrel wondering that perhaps she should have used trash bags, but that meant a trip to the store and she chose not to go out into public.

"Looks like you have a choice to make, doesn't it? What to do with the barrel?" So lost in thought, she turned before realizing who the voice belonged to. "Hello, Amanda." Jake's smile was on his lips but the eyes held sadness. She hadn't heard him drive up. "How are you?" When she didn't reply, he said, "Better, it seems or you wouldn't be out here raking leaves." In one move, he had the barrel moving toward his truck. "I'll take these out to the farm and dump them and bring your barrel back tomorrow." He had the barrel into the back of his truck and left before she pulled her wits together.

She went through an hour of chastisement. "Serves me right. What was I thinking? But I can't stay in the house forever." Now she prayed it would rain in hopes he forgot to bring back the barrel. She stayed inside the next day although there were leaves remaining to be raked. She kept the garage door down and the drapes pulled at the windows. Some time after five o'clock, she heard a vehicle stop out front and through a crack in the drapes saw Jake returning the barrel. He didn't come to the door, but taking a rake from the back of his truck, Jake began to rake the remaining leaves from the corner of the lawn. He dumped them in the barrel and left as the day before without so much as a hello.

A bit of frustration capped with anger that he dared take such liberty on her property ignited and spewed at first; he meant well, she supposed but what was his motive? If he had told her he planned to marry, she might forgive him, at least thank him for finding her and saving her life, but she thought he was a better man than to lead her on. She had known when she was rescued, it had to have been Jake. She remembered being held and the words he crooned that only she and he could hear, yes, she remembered, they were a lifeline to one drowning. She was that tired and vaguely she knew someone else was driving, but somewhere in the time when she was found and the next two weeks she fought to live, for him and Abby, for all the good things. All hope was dashed that day, within hours of her body beginning to come alive and no one knew, certainly not the two who stood at the end of the bed when one said, "Did you not know Jake and I are getting married; he has tried to let this one down easy."

Had she handled the hurt or merely bottled it up to take out and examine over and over, making herself sick at heart, threatening to disrupt healing to her body? She had to turn loose of it. There was more than personal suffering. There was the joy Abby brought day by day, all the innocence shared in being loved unconditionally. When Jake married, her time with Abby would be over. Was he trying to condition her to seeing him because he planned to continue to bring Abby to her mother as Abby's sitter?

On the third day he returned around the same time, storing the barrel in the back and then to take a ladder from his truck and come to the front where she had left several strings of lights dangling. He was there a short time and then putting the ladder back in his truck drove away. She could not fathom why he was doing this. Surely the one he was engaged to would complain. One thing she found difficult; she could not rightly persuade herself to embrace the fact another woman was marrying the man who first ask her to marry him. For that, she berated herself, it was her fault, she had lingered thinking the hurt Clark created in her might be passed on to him. Now she knew true sadness in what she had done. Jake was not Clark.

Two weeks until Christmas, her father mentioned most of the farms around were preparing to close shop the next week in order to give employees time with their families. "I guess Jake will be keeping Abby, won't he?" Because of her dread of being out in public she had not shopped for gifts for Abby and her parents. In the next week, before Abby was gone, she had to face one of her fears.

By Wednesday, Amanda had the courage to drive into the city. She chose early morning thinking few would rise that early to shop. She found the gifts she wanted for her parents and headed to the children's shop around the corner. The clothes were adorable. The lady was ringing up her purchases when someone grabbed her from behind, shock registered on the clerk's face, as Amanda slumped and went limp in his arms. Later, after being revived, she remembered hearing a voice say, Mom, Mom, but she didn't know it was the one holding her. The shop owner came, Security arrived and a very forlorn looking young man in uniform was setting to one side with a woman that reminded Amanda of herself.

When he saw she was fully aware of her surroundings, he came forward, "Ma'am, I am truly sorry. I was told my mother would be here." He stumbled around in explaining, "I called home and my sister said my mother was here buying a gift." He was visibly shaken, as was Amanda. "Ma'am, please, come meet my mother." He reached for her hand and led her to where his mother stood to be introduced. "I haven't seen my mother in almost two years and I was so excited to see her. I thought you were her."

Amanda couldn't bear to see his mother crying. "Yes, ma'am, I'm his mother. Are you going to press charges?" She motioned they should sit. "I'm sure he will never try to surprise me...or mistake me...."

"Thank you for serving," she said to the young man and to his mother, "No, no, I won't but I'd like to explain. Less than two months past, I was abducted and left tied to a tree in a forest while it rained and the weather turned cold and I almost didn't come out of it, so when his arms went around me, I guess..."

"Oh, my," fresh tears appeared in the mother's eyes. "I'm so sorry." The young man looked as though he felt miserable. "He likes being in service," the mother continued, "press charges, if you must."

"What's your name?" The young man started to apologize again.

"Mary Stegal and my son, Jeremy," the woman replied."

"Mary Stegal, Jeremy, let's put this behind us. We may never see each other again, but we are friends." They hugged each other, Security left and the shop owner hand her a twenty-dollar coupon. Trying for all the world to appear calm and collected, Amanda intended to make her way to her Jeep and she was almost there when a teenager taking a driving test nearly ran her down. There was a bench behind her, and very shaken, Amanda sit, with her package by her side and her head in her hands.

That's when Jake saw her, as he was coming out of the main building on Town Square where he had been to sign papers. "Amanda? Amanda." He was coming toward her as fast as he could manage, in a half-run. "Amanda," already he could see she was white as a sheet. "Are you ill? Here, let me help you." She was rising, thinking to get to her Jeep. Taking a moment to locate it, Jake took her by the arm and ushered her to it, seeing she was in the passenger side and he under the steering wheel. "I'll drive you home." She didn't protest, any minute she was sure she was going to lose the roll she had for breakfast. As he started the Jeep, the Shop owner pecked on the window, "I saw the whole thing, but she just experienced a surprise in my shop." She explained. "That's settled but it wasn't good for her."

"Thank you," Jake said, backing out of the spot and heading toward her home. "Are you going to be all right?" Amanda nodded. She was speechless.

"All I wanted to do was buy something. I...I..." She laid her head back and closed her eyes.

Jake was thinking, God does work in mysterious ways, his wonders to perform. Just that morning he prayed, "Lord, I'm lonely to see Amanda and know she's all right." Maybe she wasn't completely all right, but he had been granted the request. He began to whistle.

"You don't have to be so cheerful," Amanda said, sounding churlish. "I'm still alive."

Jake burst out laughing. "Yes, you are and I'm glad."

"I bet," she said, just above a whisper. "I bet. Why aren't you married?"

"I don't quite understand the question but to give my best answer, it takes time."

"I'm sorry. I was out of line. I shouldn't have said any of that. Thank you for driving me home." He pulled into the drive, pressed a button and the garage door went up. She was out of the car and going into the house by the time he turned off the ignition. When he thought to deliver the keys, the door was locked. Grinning, he placed the keys on the step, put the garage door down and left. If he was lucky, someone he knew would come along. She was going to hate herself when she figured out, he walked and she talked. Jake whistled as he headed back to get his truck and a neighbor stopped to give him a ride.

The next day she drove to her mother's, with hopes Abby would be there. "Momma." Abby came to meet her, as fast as her little toddling feet would go.

"What have you been up to?" Phyllis was hanging the last wreath at the dining room windows. She studied her daughter. "Have you seen Jake, lately?"

"Why would you ask?"

"Well, he was here to drop off Abby and he was completely different than I've seen him lately. He was smiling and actually whistling as he went out the door. I wondered what made him happy for a change."

"Has Jake been unhappy? I understood he was getting married."

"Then why was he at the hospital to see you so often? I thought he cared about you."

"Now, you know." Their eyes met and nothing more was said, but Amanda resolved to leave before Jake picked up Abby. "Mom, everything looks beautiful," she kissed Phyllis and Abby. "Bye little Boo Boo," and Abby said, "Momma," and pat Amanda's face. Phyllis just shook her head.

Driving away, Amanda had a new resolve. She was getting stronger. It was time to face her demons. Sunday arrived. Five minutes before the service began, she slipped into the pew to sit with her father. Charles hugged her and said, "I'm glad you're here. Mom will be, too." From her place at the piano, Phyllis smiled and her eyes were beaming happiness to see her daughter.

The service went as usual, Deacon Baumgarten gave his long prayer, looking afterwards quite the benevolent as his eyes scanned the congregation, but landing on Amanda, he remembered the not to nice things he had said about her and as their eyes met, Amanda held firm, her eyes locked with his. Charles was watching the exchange and wondered if that was the last of it but it was Baumgarten who looked away. He smiled at his wife at the piano, our girl is coming along, the smile relayed. She's good.

Going home with her parents, she thought how comfortable it was and so like life before the divorce. How many people, she wondered, correct the mistake they made and start over. Would she have had opportunity to ask Jake to forget she had lost sight of the reward, to be loved by him the rest of her life. Oh, that there was another chance for them, but he was to marry Belinda.

They were seated at the table when Amanda's cell buzzed. "Mr. Ferguson. James?" She stepped away from the table. "You are?" surprise registered in her voice and on her face. "Well, yes, come on by." She gave him her parents address and sit down with a shush to the chair. "Forgive me, I am surprised. That is the man I told you about. The one that owned the motel, and well, he's here, coming here, I hope you don't mind. He said no one told him how I'm doing and he came to see for himself. How about that? He came for the evening and will be going back tonight."

In the following days, she had time to reflect on Mr. Ferguson's visit and the warmth with which her parents extend hospitality and friendship and it was all good but the one question she could not answer, where is Clark Benson, as Mr. Ferguson worried over her, too. All that she could surmise was that Clark's family was either hiding him or he was in rehab. Whatever, she prayed Clark was finished with her. Life was looking up. She was going to enjoy Christmas for the first time since she was twelve years old and her parents' divorce. Only one other desire of her heart would make it perfect. She would have to buckle down and forget Jake ever existed in her life but how was she going to do that loving his daughter.

She wrapped the gifts, arriving at the photos she had printed and left in the envelope wondering if Jake would ever see them. She doubted, he seldom took pictures of Abby. That was an idea, she could give these from Abby to Jake. She had a book made for Abby with Phyllis and Charles and those very special to her own heart of her and Abby when Phyllis took the picture. All that would end when Jake married but she and Phyllis could keep those photos to give Abby when she was grown.

Often she wondered that life could be so confusing, what you thought would be never happened, and then there were many situations to contend with. It was not a happy situation to think Abby would be hurt. Nothing could become clearer, than when she attended the church Christmas program, not once thinking Jake would be there. Now, his absence was understood. Jake had not left the church. He had helped another church until their minister of music arrived.

The last two weeks felt better, finally stepping out into the real world, the biggest shock from her shopping spree had not been the young man's mistaking her for his mother, it was Jake present to drive her home, but puzzling that he left without saying a word. And now, here Amanda stood at the punch bowl when Jake made his presence known and coming through the door was Belinda, with her eyes on Jake. Belinda, all smiles made a beeline for Jake and planted a kiss on his cheek, though it was obvious she was aiming for his lips. The church people were clapping hands and hollering. It was chaos. Amanda slipped quietly out of the building, and text her mother. "Sorry, I had to leave."

Dante called as she arrived home. "What are you doing?"

"Very little. I just left a party. Why?"

"I've been trying to reach you. There's a Gala, on Bonn street, a bit posh if I do say so, but I need a partner. Would you go with me? I've called all day but your phone goes to voice mail."

"What do I wear?"

"Do you have anything festive and a bit far out?"

She laughed. "You can be the judge. See you when you get here."

"How quick can I pick you up?"

"It will take me every bit of ten minutes max."

"What? Get outta here. No woman has ever said that before. I'm on my way."

"My goodness, Miss Molly." Dante stepped inside and walked a circle around her. "You already had that little piece of thread?" She was laughing and nodding at the same time. He did a little rumba. "We gonna win this one, wait and see."

"Based on dancing or this dress?" She asked.

"Both. Ma deah, you look ravishing." He was opening the door. "Don't know who let you get away..."

"I didn't know there was a dance floor on Bonn."

"They opened it up for whatever is going on with the city. It was the suit factory, now it is wine and dine, white table cloth, waiter, and dance. The works. High dollar. Getting quite a name, too."

"Are you going to be dancing?"

"We are going to be dancing. You don't want to waste that dress."

"Oh, no, my friend. I don't do contest."

He was laughing as he parked one block away from where she remembered the old suit factory. "Come, along, Chickie, we are gonna jive tonight." She was still standing. He back stepped took her arm and said, "Oh, all right, we will practice right here. The music goes chu chu chu cha chu cha chu chu, you stand still, swing your hips and that dress does the work. Try it."

"Like this?"

"Yeah, but no eye rolling please it makes people think you don't like me." He grinned, taking her arm. "The second step, I stand still, music changes key, you do a dance around me. We win the prize and split it. Okay?"

"Sure. Five dollars will buy a banana split, won't it?"

"Maybe, but five hundred will buy a lot of ice cream."

They had been there an hour and the contest was turning out professional dancers, while Amanda became quite nervous and then their names were called. "Remember, let the dress do the talking. We got this." He whispered in her ear, "smile, no matter what happens."

She was a little stiff. As if it was part of their routine, Dante leaned back, hand on his chin as if thinking, and then stepped forward and pulled the pin that held her hair up and the crowd went wild. After that, beginning to think they might have a chance, Amanda gave her all.

"The winner is." The next thing she knew, Dante was hugging her, lifting her up and swinging her around. The crowd loved them. When he stood her firmly on the floor, not three feet away, Amanda looked into Jake's eyes and his expression was grim. Amanda's smile turned stubborn seeing Belinda step by his side and loop her arm through Jake's. It flashed through her mind, if he was music leader at the church, he shouldn't be here, in an environment that sold liquor, and a small voice echoed, neither should you.

Dante felt the change. "Amanda, do you need to go home." She nodded. "Okay," he said, "I'll get the check and we will leave." He was concerned but he had seen Jake on the way out and it appeared he and the lady were in a deep discussion.

Standing in the shadows, a lone stranger watched through the window as Jake Turner and the black-haired lady talked. It seemed more of a heated discussion but then, she may have been more demonstrative. He liked her looks. This wasn't his territory he was just passing through. He knew the car she arrived in, fast behind the guy in the pickup truck; he thought he recognized him, and he was right. He was the kind, tried to impress his own strait-laced ways off anyone that would listen. He found the woman far more interesting and made his way toward her car. She would be an easy win.

"Amanda, I worry about you. You've got to either let him go or set down and talk with him."

"Why, Dante? He didn't waste any time connecting with her."

"We don't know that. Sometimes things aren't what they seem, and I know Jake. He's a good man."

"I thought that too, until he talked one way to me and then was with her the next time, I saw him."

"Maybe he was trying to turn loose of her. I gave you, her history."

"Well, maybe you should have given it to Jake Turner. I doubt he'd believe it."

Depressed over seeing Jake with Belinda, once she was home, Amanda went to bed. She had been two places and neither had left her feeling content. She wondered, why did Jake have such a smoldering expression?

Chapter
11

·······································

T wo days before Christmas, Amanda's order was delivered early morning. Along with a few items necessary to a farm employee's life, she put a pair of leather gloves in the sacks according to the size her dad thought each man would wear. In a large burlap bag, she disguised the round ice chest that held drinks. Charles agreed to pick up the snack trays and Phyllis was bringing the desert she found through the years the men liked best. The day they closed down for Christmas everyone agreed to return for two hours out of their busy schedule on the twenty third of December.

Hiring Woodsey's son to drive the rented car had been the hardest trick to carry out in the scheme of the whole gathering. "You'll have to dress like an elf," she reminded him, "and keep our secret." A grin had spread across his face as he assured her, he could do it. Now, it was time to put everything into motion. Charles and Phyllis were to arrive first and then in complete Christmas wear, Amanda and Woodsey's son. "Easiest fifty-dollar bill I have ever made," he said. Amanda replied, "Don't be so sure."

"Miss Amanda, is that you?" Robert's eyes were on the door to the house, not believing this Santa figure could possibly be his father's employer, Miss Amanda Lanis. He was getting antsy not knowing what to do.

Amanda tried her deep belly laugh on Robert. "Yes, Mr. Elf, it's me and I'm burning up. Help me load up this stuff." Her fake round belly was getting in the way. "Just put the basket of gifts in the back seat." Once everything was loaded, she tried getting in the front. "Oh, me, am I going to have to lay in the back seat?" But they made it and the shop was rocking and rolling with fun Christmas music. She gave Robert his instructions, lastly saying, "If I signal to stop or slow down, please do, I may be trying to have a stroke." The men appeared glad to be together and at first count she found everyone present.

Robert announced, 'Everyone form a line to see Santa. Santa's going to make you happy, but don't be mean to Santa. Santa's taking down what you want for Christmas. Be nice and then we will eat." Phyllis and Charles in his wheel chair with Abby on his lap were ready for the men. The two didn't have a game plan but the men loved the atmosphere they brought with them and baby Abby was adorable as a little angel but she kept reaching for Amanda saying, "Momma."

"I believe we can guess who is Santa," Dante called out. "If that's Miss Phyllis and our boss man, then I believe Santa might be our boss, Miss Amanda. We know because that baby keeps reaching out." Everyone was clapping, "But we don't know the elf."

"Elf forgot to change his tennis shoes," Woodsey announced. "Robert, you like being an elf?"

The two hours were up before they realized the evening was getting late and Amanda insist, they return home to spend time with their family. Everyone was laughing as Amanda pulled off the mask and toboggan hat and let her hair spill free. Charles hand out the bonus to each employee and then Amanda gave every man a hug and passed out the gift sacks. "How did you think to do this?" Dante asked.

"I always wanted to and it seemed perfect with dad's employees, so much fun, I couldn't resist."

"Merry Christmas, Amanda." Dante bent down to place a kiss on her cheek and she hugged him.

Woodsey and Robert were the last to leave. Amanda put a fifty-dollar bill in Robert's hand and thanked him. It was after they all left and her parents were ready to go, too, that she realized home was going to be really lonely. It was hitting hard; she couldn't face going home to an empty house.

Phyllis sensed the melancholy in her child and persuaded her to go home with them. "You can leave when you want but I have cookies to make and you can watch Abby, although as much as she has been passed around, I'd say a bath and nap are in order. Amanda found herself in charge, running Abby's bath and watching her play in the water and then into fresh pajamas and settling into Amanda's arms as they sit in the rocking chair with Abby taking a bottle. No one heard the door open as Charles was asleep with the television running.

Phyllis turned to find Jake standing at her elbow, watching the cookie making process first hand. "Oh," she was startled to turn and find him there. She put a finger to her lips and motioned he was to follow. "Don't let Amanda know you've seen this or she will go home, fast as can be. Okay?" Jake nodded. Sitting in the chair, Amanda's back was to the door. "Now, listen."

Jake watched. Abby would remove the bottle, pat Amanda's face and say, "momma." Amanda's head was bowed as she kissed the top of Abby's head. "Bye Bye, baby, don't you cry," Amanda was singing. "Daddy's gonna buy Momma a wedding ring. Bye Bye, baby, don't you cry." Jake listened. It was when Amanda put Abby on her shoulder to burp and Abby got excited seeing her daddy, that Phyllis had to think up a plan as Jake made a hasty two step to the kitchen.

She handed a box to Jake, "Would you run to the store for me? I need two of this, please."

As he left, she called to Amanda, "Will it be all right, with you, if Jake comes in to collect his baby?"

"I didn't realize it was time, Mother." Amanda joined Phyllis in the kitchen with Abby hanging over her arm. "This one didn't sleep, at all, but I guess she will tonight." She gave Abby into Phyllis arms and pecked a kiss on their cheeks, adding one for her daddy, on the way out.

Arriving home, she noticed a glass container of red roses on the door step. "In this weather, with it supposed to snow," she muttered, getting out of the car. Looking around cautiously, she scooped them into her arms and let the garage door down and hurried inside the house. "Who would do this?"

She tried watching television but with a season of new shows she could not find one of interest. She mopped the kitchen floor, though it didn't really need it. Pacing around the house, tweaking first one Christmas ornament, then another; and making sure all the lights worked, it was the first time she missed the string of lights on the front of the house that Jake had fixed. Pulling on a heavy jacket, she went out to check the problem, but they weren't there; the lights were completely gone.

That didn't make sense. She backed up, nearly to the street. With the tree lit up and her room cozy, she had to admit it looked beautiful, and the lights that were missing would have been the icing on the cake. "Just my luck she muttered." Her phone buzzed but she didn't answer. She wasn't in the mood.

"Well, I can't fix anything in the dark." As quickly as she spoke, she looked around to see if anyone heard her. "Of course, they didn't," she said, answering that thought. "Oh, my goodness, now I'm talking to myself, it's that bad." She glanced toward her neighbors' homes. "They have company. It's almost Christmas and I'm standing out in the street talking to myself and if they hear me, they will think I'm crazy." Going in, she shouted, "I'm glad my neighbors on both sides have guest. IT's Christmas." And she hurried in and shut the door. She was having her very own pity party.

She sit down, thinking to read, but that wasn't making her happy tonight. Her mind was on Jake's terrible thunderous expression the last time she saw him, and then Abby came to mind, patting her face and saying, "momma." She neither encouraged or discouraged Abby calling her momma." Once, she heard a noise and went to the window to investigate what had fallen but there was nothing. And then it was bedtime. She decided to leave the lights on. There were still pills to take from the hospital stay, but she needed a drink of water.

The light switch was just inside the door. As she reached out to flip it on she felt a huge hand cover hers. "Dad? How did you get here?" When the man tried to kiss her, she knew it wasn't dad. "Clark."

He was pulling her close. "I know you missed me," he said into her ear. "I've been getting recharged for you and me. There's no telling what we learn when we listen and I've been listening but I had to come back for you." He laughed, "Why are you moving like you don't like me. Stop."

Amanda felt fear pump through her veins. She heard the warning in his voice. There was no way she could overcome him; he was too tall and if she needed it the gun was not even close. She prayed he didn't find it. She had to act normal. "When did you get here?"

"Does that matter? I came for you. I told you to stay there."

"Stay where?"

"In Grampa's house. He was going to marry us."

"Was I at your Grampa's house?" She moved back as far as he allowed.

"You know you were. Then I tied you to a tree to punish you. Now, we are going back."

She shivered, thinking she couldn't face that again. She had to get to the gun. But could she do it, make him believe she would shoot him? His hand on hers became tighter, hurting but she wouldn't cry out. She had to make him think she was his friend. She felt her phone in the jacket pocket and wondered if he realized it was there. If she could dial the Police number, she had to have the phone silenced.

"You seem tired. Don't we need to rest before we go?"

Crooking his arm around her neck he brought her under his arm. "What are you trying to pull?"

"Don't you remember? We talked about a nice Christmas with Christmas Carols, maybe going to see a children's program and having time together to reflect on the true reason for Christmas. We could watch a movie."

"I went along with you, didn't I? But you said, this time you weren't buying my favorite gift. You said you never wanted to see me again but I knew you didn't mean it." He began to laugh, and it was a fiendish sound. His eyes had taken on a look she well remembered. It meant very soon there would be no reasoning or small talk at all. He was working himself into a frenzy and during that time, before, she was tied to the tree and left to die. She knew it was coming, when he said, "I believe you know I have to punish you, so you won't do this kind of thing again." He slapped her, and as her head snapped back, her body followed and she would have fallen but for his strong hold on her arm.

Her right hand in the jacket pocket clamped down on the phone and she prayed to God, please let whatever I'm pressing land on the phone number to the Police station. Only a miracle would bring the results she desperately needed. He had lost comprehension of time and place. He had become a mad man. When he slapped her the second time, she slid to the floor, wishing to die before he killed her.

"I ought to set this house on fire with you in it," he screamed. "Get up." But she couldn't, not yet.

When he thought to pick her up, she slid away, scrambled to get onto her feet and ran toward the bedroom. He was a step behind as she tried to shut the door, but he grabbed it and slammed it against her, knocking her near the bed and flat of her back as pain shot through her body. She thought her ribs were crushed but if she had any strength left, if she had one chance it was now. She pushed with her feet, going under the bed, grappling for the box where she had hidden the gun. Unable to see anything in the dark space, but his feet, she pulled the trigger and let go, sending the bullet a straight line somewhere between the calf of his leg and ankle. She knew, he was hit, by the scream and the thud on the floor as he cried out in pain. No doubt he heard the click of the gun and was able to move out of range as she prepared to shoot again. She heard other noises, as if he had fallen into a piece of furniture but she was quiet, unsure if he would return with a weapon of his own. It seemed an eternity she lay there, listening for movement, but it did not come. Still, she dare not leave the safety of the bed, even if she was able. He would kill her rather than admit defeat. She could not move for fear.

It seemed an hour, she heard movement through the house. The quiet of heavy silence broken only by a slight touch of a foot set down, coming closer. With quivering hands, she held the gun, ready once more to defend herself and just as a light went on from behind the door, she realized he would not know where the switch was installed, there was another one in the house. She readied the gun and as she faded into oblivion it seemed someone called her name but darkness overcome her.

They picked her up from the floor, after dissembling the bed, while outside, the two Police cars lights were flashing as they loaded Clark Benson into the back seat of one preparing to take him in to Emergency for a gunshot wound to the leg. Already he had called his mother and she had given the Police officers orders as to how her son should be treated if they didn't want a law suit on their hands.

Amanda was loaded into the ambulance. The attendants were unsure what had happened to her. It appeared she either had bruised or broken ribs, determined by the pain she was experiencing. The gun that was used to shoot Clark Benson was confiscated, only for the time being, because she had a permit.

Her parents were on the way to the hospital. Jake Turner was already there, having been tipped off by one of his friends on the Police Force. He was pacing, the result of severe anxiety over Amanda's unknown condition. Abby was entertaining the Medical staff of Jericho Hospital. She was always in her daddy's eye-view as she sit in the stroller.

Phyllis was driving as fast as she was talking. Charles was listening. "I can't believe what Clair told me today. It seems Belinda told all around town that she and Jake were getting married in the new year." She glanced at Charles to be sure he was listening. "Are you getting this?" Charles nodded, "Yes, Phyllis, I assume there's more."

Satisfied, Phyllis continued. "I am wondering if that is why Amanda quit seeing Jake." Charles nodded, "Could be." Taking a deep breath, Phyllis said, "But it was a lie. Clair's nephew was at that new restaurant they put in on Bonn Street, you know, where the suit factory used to be. It appears, Dante ask Amanda to be his partner in the dance contest. Remember? She left us the night Belinda showed up and kissed Jake on the cheek? Well, our Amanda left, then Jake left and last of all Belinda hi-tailed it down to Bonn Street and tried to show ownership of Jake and according to Brent, Clair's nephew, Jake told her to take a hike, that he was not interested in her, never was but had tried to be kind to her and it did nothing but cause a problem between him and our Amanda."

Charles smiled. Whether at Phyllis or because he thought in time Amanda would see what a fine man Jake Turner was. He was appreciating Phyllis more every day. He didn't know why in the heck he got side tracked with Bertha all those years back and wasted precious time with his family. But they'd come together loving little Abby, which was another reason Amanda and Jake had to work things out.

"Here we are," Phyllis said. "I'll drive you under the portico, can you manage if I get a wheel chairand sit you right inside until I park?"

"Yes, I'll be just fine and I'm sorry that you have to do all this." Their eyes met. "Thank you."

"I'm glad to," she replied. "I'm so glad we are together, when things like this happen." He agreed.

⚜

Jake saw Phyllis pushing Charles in a wheelchair and went to meet them. "I hope you don't mind my being here?" His eye was on Abby, feet on the floor, pushing and trying to move, but seeing Charles was with her daddy, she went into a tail spin, jabbering away, which pleased Charles, immensely.

The doctor came out and Jake went to meet him. "Is she okay?" The doctor put out a hand, as he nodded. "Let me tell this information to all of you one time. How's that?" Jake agreed.

"Okay," he made note of Phyllis and Charles. "It seems there's an element of surprise that Amanda was picked up, but that's part of a stalker's plan. We are just fortunate it was here and all is well." He gave them a satisfied sigh. "It is our opinion that Amanda may have broken ribs. We have wrapped her torso pretty good. She can't reach for a few days…so I'd say she needs to stay home, a few days, with someone or at least check on her." He smiled, "And why she fainted. She gets excited or, too deep a feeling to explain, as in, she said she was anxious and we used smelling salt, and you will need to keep a bag of it handy, just in case. Your daughter has been through a lot and as a survivor of a stalker, I think we all realize what could have happened. The Lord looked after your daughter." He started to leave them and then added, "Let's keep it quiet for her a day or two, don't worry her with trivial things."

Amanda saw her parents but when asked if she would like to see Jake, she shook her head and said, "no." Glancing at the calendar on the wall, she said, "I don't know that I'm staying. Clark's in Police custody and of that means I'll be safe." One glance at her parent's expression and she added, "I'm not dying. I was hurt, but people leave ER many days with wrapped ribs, because they're never sure, if they're bruised or broken. Right?" She tried to give them her best reassuring smile. "Now, go home. It's Christmas Eve, I'll be fine."

"You wanted a Christmas with family together, decorations and people that love the Lord," Phyllis said, wistfully. "Remember? You said that when your dad and I divorced and it seemed to stay as you grew to be an adult. Now, we're together?" A tear slid down Phyllis cheek. "We let you down, but I couldn't stay with the circumstance."

"No, she couldn't," Charles added. "It was my fault. Your mother was everything you needed when I failed you." His voice became husky.

"I know, Dad," Amanda reached for their hands. "Let's don't blame anyone, I'm getting three out of four, so I can't complain…it's strange you all remember me saying that. I was a kid and home was where the two of you were, and our house decorated, I loved it, but after the divorce those first two years Mom didn't have the heart to do it…now she does." Amanda smiled at them. "Come on, you two."

"What was the fourth thing?" Charles asked. "I didn't know there was a wish list."

"A husband, I think," Phyllis added. "A Christian man, wasn't it?" Amanda wasn't smiling, as she whispered, yes. "Don't be sad, honey. You have a long life ahead of you and you were young."

"Maybe, but Mom, I messed up something terrible thinking Clark was, because in the beginning he appeared to be…but it was when I realized he wasn't and left, the stalking began." She took a deep breath, "he couldn't take anyone saying no to him and that's why he followed me here."

Phyllis hugged her daughter. "It's over. God was watching over you. Now it's time to move forward."

"He was a wolf in sheep's clothing, Hon." Charles wheeled to the door. "Now, rest until you know what you are going to do. I love you. See you tomorrow."

◌∽

They had barely cleared the hall when Amanda called the nurse's station and ask if her doctor was still in the building. "If he is," she said, "Please tell him I need to see him. Thank you."

Next, she called Dante. By the time they were bringing in the evening meals, Amanda had the release papers and was sitting in Dante's truck on her way home. "Thank you so much, Dante."

He grinned, "That's what friends are for and by the way, I owe you your half of the dance win."

"That was hard to believe, wasn't it? But it was a jivey tune we danced to."

"From what I'm hearing, you were the pick. You made that dress do the trick and you looked beautiful."

"Why, Dante, thank you. It's a wonder I even had a dress, I left so quick, I didn't bring much."

"I'm glad you brought the red dress." He grinned. "Let's do it again. It will be a few months."

"So, do you have plans for tomorrow? You do realize it's Christmas?"

"First I'm going to Mass and then I have a dinner date with a wonderful family."

"I'm happy to hear that. I would hate to think anyone would be alone on Christmas."

He was quiet a moment and then said, "Amanda, Jake and Abby have nowhere to go."

She gave a gasp of surprise. "Why?" What happened to Belinda and Jake?"

"There was never anything to it. I found out today, she lied to make you feel bad. In fact, she lied to everyone, all over town and in the church and now it's said she is telling she threw Jake over for some one else."

"Is this for real, Dante? Because if it is, I have been so wrong about Jake when my own heart was breaking. I couldn't understand how he changed and I decided it was her influence."

"You remember the night we danced and won?" She nodded. "That was not so long ago. They were having some kind of discussion and Jake looked angry and she was putting her hand on him as if to keep him from showing by his actions just how angry he was. He found out about her lies."

"Why didn't he tell me?"

"Did he have an opportunity? Benson was watching you and you were staying out of Jake's sight, trying to handle your own heart ache. I wondered if you had made your parents stay mum about where you were. Jake told me your mother cried when she said she couldn't invite him to Thanksgiving or Christmas dinners because they would not hurt you more than Benson already had and they didn't know the truth about why you two weren't seeing each other."

"Dante, what must I do?"

"I kind of get the feeling you two love each other but you're just too blame stubborn to work together." He saw the misery register on her face. "We don't often get a second chance, Amanda." He saw the tears roll down her cheeks. "Want me to drop you off there?"

Jake sit Abby in her bouncy seat and for a minute she wasn't happy. Now that she was walking, that was all she wanted to do. He finished towel drying his hair and pulled on a long-sleeved T. Abby had pajamas with the feet in and he wasn't sure what she thought about them as she kept looking down and moving her feet as if they belonged to someone else. "You are one funny, little girl," he said. "And if I didn't have you, what would I do?" He sit on one end of the sofa and watched her try to come across the room. "That's not your walker, Sissy. I'm afraid it's stationary." He tossed her a small stuffed penguin. "Here you go, short stuff." Abby laughed.

He thought he saw lights and watched as a truck backed up and left the drive. "I guess they were turning around," he said. But the door bell was ringing. "That's unusual," he said getting up. He opened the door and looked straight out to the road and saw no one. Just as he started to close it, he got a glimpse of someone standing to one side, almost in the shadow.

Amanda's heart was thumping in her chest. This would be the most important question of her life. "Why aren't you married?"

Jake did a double take. "Amanda?" He almost lost his cool. "What are you doing out in this weather? Don't you know it's turning colder by the minute?" He stepped to the porch and held out a hand for her to come up the steps. "Why?"

"I had things I needed to do."

"But I heard the doctor say you aren't to be out, nor lift, and to keep it quiet for a few days."

"Are you and Abby too noisy for me to come in?"

Amanda standing at the doorstep was much more than he ever expected. He had lost his manners and hospitality, to boot. "Come in." Now she took his hand and stepped inside.

Abby was standing in the bouncy seat, waiting to see who came into the room and when she saw it was Amanda, she went wild. "Momma. Momma. Momma."

"Hi, Baby, how's my girl?" Abby was holding her arms up to be taken out of the seat.

Jake was in shock. "What are you doing? Did you run out of gas, did your car break down?"

"No, I came to ask you a serious question." He leaned forward, waiting. "Why aren't you married?"

He was actually gaping. "In our early days, you ask me all the time to marry you and then we progressed to the point I think we thought we might marry, but Belinda came along and then I was abducted. Do you remember, you ask me more than once, "Will you marry me and I didn't think you knew enough about me to be satisfied, so then you said, "one day you will ask me why I'm not married and I'll tell you the woman I want won't say yes, but the day you come to me and ask again, why I'm not married…that's when we get really serious about the answer." He sit down, wondering where she was going with this, "I'm here, to ask you my last time, Jake, why aren't you married?"

"Sadly, my heart has been breaking because I don't think the woman I love wants me. Do you?"

"When I was in the forest, Jake, all I could think was, do you still want me? When I was fighting so hard to live, I prayed I would come out with a body whole enough that you would still want me and tonight, I'm here because I feel you are the only man in the world will ever make me happy. Do you still want me?"

Jake rose from the sofa and took her in his arms. "Amanda." Tears ran down his cheeks to mingle with those of Amanda's. "I have prayed for your health and ask God to help me wish you well wherever you go, whether it's here at Jericho or a city beyond. Amanda, will you marry me?" He heard her whisper yes. "It has to be soon, like next week." He was whirling her around, he was that happy.

Abby was beating the stuffed toy on the tray to the bouncy seat. "Momma," she said.

"Can you stay?" His heart was in his eyes. "I won't do anything to hurt you. You know I won't."

She smiled. "Do you still have that old jogging suit of your Mother's?"

"Merry Christmas," they said together, and for Amanda, it was the answer to years of prayers.

Amanda arrived early to help with Christmas dinner. She gave her parents a gift to enjoy in the years ahead. "Oh, it's lovely," her mother said as she opened the box to the family album, complete with a new picture of the three and a number of pictures of Abby. They were all relieved that Charles wasn't in pain on this day. Just as Amanda was about to mention Dante's news that he would be having dinner with a lovely family, the doorbell rang.

Everyone shared a hug and laughter that Phyllis had secretly ask both Dante and Jake, because she felt everything was going to be all right and when Woodsey with his wife and son arrived, their Christmas dinner seemed about perfect, until Phyllis said, "no, there's one more." Glancing out the window, Amanda saw James Ferguson coming across the lawn. Charles, taking his seat as head of the family, said, "we are about as corny as those Christmas movies we see, and doesn't it feel good?"

Phyllis came out of the kitchen long enough to check on everyone. "Jake," she said, "I believe you look better this morning. What do you suppose brought the change?" Jake reached across to hold hands with Amanda. "No words necessary," Phyllis said, beaming on the two.

That was the family dinner, friends and family. It seemed on this day; hearts beat as one. The year they were leaving behind held moments of hardship, but for Amanda this was the best Christmas since her parents' divorce. Now, she had everything she'd prayed for and more.

But Jake wasn't finished. "You haven't shone me the Christmas tree yet," he said. "And you have said, nothing was the same after your mother and Dad divorced, now they're together again and we have found each other." She led him into the room where the tree reached the ceiling and Jake went down on one knee. "Amanda, I've asked many times but this time I hope you reply. Will you marry me?" He held up a beautiful diamond for her finger, as Amanda said Yes."

"Momma," Abby said, toddling to Amanda.. Amanda scooped her up to plant a kiss on Abby's cheek and Abby pat Amanda's face and said, "momma."

The New Year fell on Sunday. The new Pastor presided over a very special wedding. Sitting behind Phyllis and Charles Lanis, Deacon Baumgarten and James Ferguson beamed proudly on the couple. "None like those two," said James, to which Baumgarten replied, "Fine people. Fine people."

Abby toddled up and down the aisle strewing rose petals while the pastor led Jake and Amanda through scripture and their own written vows. Amanda was a beautiful bride and Jake a handsome groom. It was the wedding of the year. Someone did mention, quietly behind closed doors, Belinda thought she could snag him, but that idea was never even close. She always comes out smelling like arose, one said. Now she's married to that fellow that kidnapped Amanda. His mother has more money than they know what to do with. We're sure Belinda can help with that until he gets out of jail.

THE END

BOOKS BY BETTY LOWREY

Promises

Forgiven

Forbidden

Forsaken

Forever

Forgotten

Secrets

When Somebody Loves You

For The Love Of Stormy Weather

Loving You Always

When Dreams Come True

Where There's Love

When You Call My Name

Engraved On My Heart

When My Heart Sings

A Heart Twice Blessed

Faith In Spite of the Storm

Barkley

Lily

Emma

AMANDA

CPSIA information can be obtained
at www.ICGtesting.com
Printed in the USA
JSHW021634151222
34838JS00002B/150